Lost and Found in a New World

The New World Book Four

Sherry Derr-Wille

Published by Rogue Phoenix Press, LLP

ISBN: 978-1-62420-642-9

Credits
Cover Artist: Designs by Ms G
Editor: Amanda Armstrong

Dedication

To my fans who have supported me ever since the first book was published in 2003. You all rock!

Prologue

"I don't know what I'm going to do, man," Drake Nevins confided to his best friend. "The bitch just contacted me and told me she's pregnant. I don't want to be tied down to some brat."

"I'll tell you what I think. It's best if you make yourself scarce. Once the kid is born, and we know it's a boy, we'll be able to take care of the problem. I know a place where no one will ever find him. These people don't ask questions. It will take a little work, but once we get our hands on him, we take him out to Henderson Ranch. They pay a premium for unwanted kids, especially if we say his mother is a dirty whore. Old man Henderson likes that kind of kid."

"Won't they want to know who his parents are?"

"Hell no. All they have to do is tell the state that the kid was abandoned by his mother. He'll also tell them she was nothing more than a whore, and no questions asked, they send Henderson money to raise him. Once he's eighteen, the old man will find the kid a good job down in Mexico on one of the ranches. Easy peasy, no muss, no fuss, you're off the hook and the kid gets looked after."

"How do we go about contacting this guy?"

"Leave that to me. Just lay low and don't answer any of her communications. In fact, it's best if you leave the state and disappear for about three years or so. Once the kid is past that baby stage, we'll get more money from Henderson."

Chapter One

Rita Simes walked from work to the daycare center where her three-year-old son, Peter, stayed for the hours while she worked. She regretted the fact she needed to work to support her child, but his father left as soon as he learned her child's gender. Try as she might, she couldn't find him in order to get him to pay child support.

After three years, she was content being a single parent, but she did get tired. Working long hours in order to give her son what he needed, as well as spend quality time with him, was hard. When she first told her parents she was pregnant, they'd kicked her out and she'd moved away to another city about ten miles from where she grew up, to raise her son. It took a lot of hard work, but finally she was able to get a place of her own.

Even though it was difficult, she eventually found a high paying job. One that paid enough to finance her apartment as well as pay for their daily needs and childcare.

For some reason, the closer she got to the daycare center, a feeling of dread came over her. Something was wrong, but she couldn't decide what it was.

"Good afternoon," the receptionist greeted her.

"Good afternoon. Is Peter ready to leave?"

"Didn't you know? His father picked him up about three hours ago. He said they would see you back at the apartment."

Panic struck her like a slap in the face. She hadn't heard from Drake since they learned the gender of their child. How dare he come and take her son out of daycare without her knowledge?

As fast as she could, she hailed a hovercraft taxi to take her to the apartment. After paying the fare, she rushed into the building and prayed the elevator would be faster than it usually was.

Unfortunately, the assent to the tenth floor seemed to take forever. As soon as the door opened, she hurried into the darkened apartment. Switching on a light, she could tell someone had been there. Her sense of the security the cameras had given her in the past was shattered. Just yesterday she'd been informed that for some unknown reason it was no longer working.

She continued to look around the apartment with trepidation. She'd been violated. All of Peter's clothes and toys were missing. On the table was a note in Drake's scrawl.

You've kept my son from me long enough. He's with me now instead of his mother who is a whore. Don't look for us because you won't find us. Drake.

Tears rolling down her cheeks, she immediately activated her communicator to call the authorities.

Within minutes, two police officers were at her door. She was in a state of shock when they told her that since the boy had been taken by his biological father, there wasn't anything they could do. With the new laws, each parent, neglectful or not could claim custody. Considering she had no idea how to find Drake, she soon learned she didn't have a leg to stand on. Her son had been taken from her and she knew she'd never see him again.

~ * ~

"I'm your father," Drake told a bewildered Peter. "We're going on an adventure. I even have a brand-new hovercraft to take us there."

"I want my mommy," Peter cried.

The more the boy cried, the madder Drake got. How could his son be crying about his bitch of a mother? Well, he'd get over that soon enough.

Without hesitation, he reached over and backhanded the boy. It must have shocked him into compliance because his wails turned to frightened whimpers.

His friend, Delos, waited for him at the transfer point, just outside of Missoula, Montana. “Are you sure this is going to work?”

“Everything is set. Henderson is willing to pay us thirty thousand dollars for the brat, twenty thousand for you and ten thousand for me. I’ll meet you back here in three days to make the split.”

Drake agreed, knowing full well there wouldn’t be a split. As far as he was concerned, Delos wasn’t the brightest bulb in the box. It would be easy to dispose of him once he returned with the money. He’d lived in the Missoula area for over two years and knew there was enough wilderness where he could dispose of the body and it wouldn’t be found for weeks, or probably even years. No matter what, he would be long gone. By the end of the week, he would be living like a king somewhere far away from Montana.

~ * ~

“Are you taking me to my mommy?” Peter whined.

“You’re going to have a new home, brat. Your mother is a dirty whore and she’s not fit to raise a child.”

Peter cried, silently, afraid this strange man would hit him, like the man who said he was his father. He didn’t know what a dirty whore was, but it must not have been good if these men were taking him away from her.

The hovercraft landed and a man who towered over Peter came to greet them. “Is this the new one?” he asked.

“Yes, he’s in good health and out of diapers. I know you prefer to get them young.”

“You’re right. What about the mother?”

“She’s a whore and not fit to raise such a fine young man. I know you’ll take good care of him.”

The big man got down on one knee and looked Peter in the eye. “What’s your name, boy?”

“P-Peter,” he stammered.

“You’ll like it here. There are a lot of boys for you to play with and you’ll be learning a trade. There will be lots of fresh air and you’ll grow into a responsible young man.”

Peter watched as the big man handed Delos some money and guided him away from the hovercraft and to a nasty looking building which he called the dormitory.

Before entering the building, Peter looked back to see the hovercraft lift off and disappear into the lengthening shadows of late afternoon.

Inside the dormitory, he was led to a bunk bed and told it was where he was going to sleep. On the bunk next to his was a boy about the same age as himself.

"This is Christopher. He hasn't got no folks, either."

"I got a momma," Peter protested.

"You're here because your mama is like all women, she's a dirty whore. Women like her ain't fit to raise kids. You're better off here."

~ * ~

It was dark when Delos landed in Missoula. Even though it was earlier than they'd agreed to meet, he found Drake waiting for him.

"How did it go?" Drake asked.

"Smooth as silk. Henderson never balked at the agreed upon price."

"It's too late to go back to our place and celebrate. I rented us a room at the hotel. We can party all night and not have to clean up the mess in the morning."

The thought of free alcohol made Delos' mouth water. Ever since they embarked on this transaction, he'd stayed sober. He looked forward to a good drink.

~ * ~

Drake let the booze flow freely until Delos was so drunk, he passed out. Knowing this was his chance, he took the pillow from his bed and held it over his friend's face until he was dead. By suffocating Delos, there would be no evidence of the crime left in the room he'd rented at the hotel. Once he was certain Delos was dead, he took the body from the room to his hovercraft and left for the remote mountain cabin where he'd been hiding out so Rita couldn't find him.

The first thing in the morning, he took off, saying goodbye to Missoula with the entire thirty thousand dollars in his pocket.

It was still early when he docked his craft at the cabin that he'd called home for the past two years. He would miss it, but he had bigger fish to fry. Once he dumped Delos' body into one of the remote ravines, he cleaned out his belongings and left his mountain hideaway forever.

~ * ~

"Have you seen Delos Reynolds?" Evelyn asked, as she served breakfast to one of the deputy sheriff's officers who stopped by her café every morning.

"Come to think of it, I haven't seen him in about a month. Haven't seen that no good friend of his, Drake Nevins, either. They were quite the pair. Reynolds didn't have the sense the One God gave a goat. As for Nevins, I always figured he was the brains of the two of them. Maybe I'll take a run out to that cabin of theirs and see what's what."

It was late afternoon when Deputy Jason Fielding returned to the café.

"What did you find, Jason?"

"No one's been there in quite a while. I did some nosing around and was told Nevins had a room at the hotel. When I checked into it, I learned Reynolds joined him shortly after he checked in. Guess the room was a total mess. The clerk told me they left either in the night or the early hours of the morning, without settling up their bill. He also said the room was filled with empty liquor bottles and bedding all over the floor, especially the pillow off the second bed. If I don't miss my guess, only one person left that hotel alive, and I doubt it was Reynolds."

"What makes you think that?"

"I found some things at the cabin that make me think only Nevins left the area. All of Reynolds' belongings were there, but there was nothing that belonged to Nevins. I did find some information that I think will be of interest. I'm not at liberty to say more but I have a feeling we should start looking for a body. Nevins' cabin is in a pretty remote area."

Evelyn worried about what all of this was leading to. She tolerated Nevins but she always felt sorry for Delos. There was definitely hero worship involved when it came to his relationship with Nevins. She'd met Drake's kind before. They came off as smart, but beneath the façade there was a mean streak a mile long. She wouldn't put anything past him.

"What did you do with Delos' belongings?" she finally asked.

"Had to leave them where they were. They are evidence after all. There wasn't much, just that ratty old coat he always wore, a pair of work boots and a few pieces of clothing. There were some papers with his name on them, but nothing you wouldn't expect to find."

Evelyn wondered what else could have been found at the cabin that Jason couldn't talk about. Since her uncle worked in law enforcement until his retirement three years ago, she knew better than to ask too many questions about the investigation.

~ * ~

A week later, Evelyn was surprised when two well-dressed men entered the café. They showed her their identification indicating they were from the FBI.

"What can you tell us about two men who were reportedly staying in this area by the names of Drake Nevins and Delos Reynolds?"

Evelyn took a deep breath. "I never trusted Nevins. I even doubt that was his real name. I know a con man when I see one. As for Delos Reynolds, that man would stand out in a rainstorm if no one told him to come into the house. There's no doubt about any intelligence he has or doesn't have."

"How long have they been living here?" the second agent asked.

"Let me think. I remember Nevins showing up in the spring of 2100. I think it was fall of that same year when Delos first came into town."

"How can you be so sure of the date?"

"That's easy. I bought this place in April of 2100. Nevins was one of my first customers. I didn't trust him then and I never had reason to change my mind. Let's just say when he was in the café, I didn't turn my back on him. I had a feeling if given the chance he would steal me blind if I didn't watch his every move."

Both men frantically typed notes on their communicators. "You've been very helpful. We talked to your sheriff and he directed us to the cabin those two shared. Tomorrow we will be scanning the entire area with our drones. Hopefully, they will be able to shed some light on what happened to Delos Reynolds."

When the agents left the café, Evelyn sunk down into one of the booths to regain her composure. Never in her wildest dreams had she ever thought she would be questioned by the FBI.

As for what the drones would find tomorrow, she had no doubt. Somewhere near to Nevins' cabin, in one of the remote ravines, they would, most certainly, find the remains of Delos Reynolds, God rest his soul.

~ * ~

Jeff Kruckenburg looked into the mirror in the bathroom of the hotel room he'd rented over the internet. As the site advertised, he had simply entered the room number onto the keypad and the keycard dropped into his hand. No muss no fuss, and no one to identify the man who entered the hotel with long hair and a beard.

It hadn't taken long for him to shave his beard and cut his hair. With his forged papers, no one would ever know he was once Drake Nevins.

The transformation had been much easier than he ever thought it would be. After he left Montana, he traded in the hovercraft he'd used when he picked up Peter at the daycare center. Rather than draw attention by purchasing one of the newer models, he opted for a used one, saying he'd decided he didn't need such a fancy vehicle.

The reflection that greeted him looked much younger than his actual thirty years of age. It was no wonder Rita had been such a willing partner when he suggested they go to bed together.

Although the thirty thousand dollars he'd received for selling

Peter to Henderson Ranch wasn't a fortune, he wasn't without means. Long before he met Rita, his father had died, leaving him a goodly sum. Rather than leaving it in the bank and taking monthly payments, he opted to take his inheritance in a lump sum.

Since the old man wasn't in the best of health, no one was surprised when he died in his sleep. There was no investigation into the death of Quinton Solomon Senior. As Quinton Junior, he'd played the part of the grieving son to the hilt.

Once he left Toronto behind for good, he became Drake Nevins. As an only child, no one questioned his wanting to take his inheritance and go elsewhere to start a new life.

The fact his mother deserted him and his father before he even entered puberty made leaving much easier. For the abuse he'd received at the hands of his father, he was entitled to the money, just as his father was entitled to be murdered to end the nightmare that was Drake's childhood.

After killing his father, he realized he rather enjoyed having the power of life and death over his victims. Had it not been for the money, he would have killed the boy, but getting the money Delos promised him made it easier to allow the boy to live. After all, he was the kid's biological father.

Before he left the rented room, he completely cleaned up all the hair from not only his head but also his beard. There was no sense in leaving any incriminating evidence linking Quinton Solomon or Drake Nevins to Jeff Kruckenburg. The way things were with DNA, he could never be too careful.

Early the next morning, he left the key for the room, as well as a generous tip for the cleaning staff, on the nightstand and took off for his next destination, Cherokee Village, Arkansas. There he would find a respectable business and close yet another chapter in his life.

~ * ~

It took almost a week for the FBI drones to find anything. When they did, Evelyn's worst fears came to light. In one of the remote ravines, they'd found the decomposing body of a man. Once they brought it into town, a DNA chip was recovered, identifying the remains as those of Delos Reynolds.

The talk at the café was about how the FBI, as well as the local authorities, had put out a 'be on the lookout' for Drake Nevins, who was now charged with murder. They also described him as having a heavy beard and long hair. It was also possible he was armed and dangerous.

Within a few days, the newer model hovercraft Nevins was known to drive was discovered in central Illinois. Unfortunately, once authorities checked it out, the new owner was no match for the man they were looking for. It was highly possible they'd come to a dead end and the murder of Delos Reynolds would become an unsolved mystery.

Even though Evelyn had no feelings for either Nevins or Reynolds, the thought of someone as gullible as Delos losing his life, saddened her.

Later that afternoon, the FBI agents were back at the café. "Have you ever seen Drake Nevins in the company of a small boy?"

"No, why do you ask?"

"When we put out the information on Nevins, we received word of the abduction of a small boy in Missouri by his father, Drake Nevins. If he kidnapped the child, it's possible he killed him as well. From what the mother reported, Nevins was the biological father of the boy. She also said he wanted nothing to do with either of them once she told him she was pregnant."

Evelyn felt as though she'd been gut punched. How could anyone kidnap their biological child and kill him? All her life, she'd been told she was psychic. Too many times in the past, her premonitions eventually were proven to be true. In this case, she would probably never know what happened to the child, but her senses told her the boy was still alive.

Chapter Two

Peter looked around the stark dormitory of Henderson Ranch. This was where the man named Delos told him he would be living from now on. He said Peter's mother was a whore, but he didn't know what that meant.

"I'm Christopher," a dark-haired boy said, coming over to Peter's bunk.

"I'm Peter. Why are you here?"

"Ain't got no folks. They died right after I was born. Why are you here?"

"They say my ma is a whore. I don't know what that means but it must be bad."

Peter turned his back on the boy he knew would soon become his friend. A small bag with a change of clothes sat on the bunk he'd been told would be his. He wanted his mother. He wanted his friends at the daycare center where we went while his mother worked. He didn't want to be here. He wished the man who called himself his father never came to the daycare center.

Remembering his father also brought to mind the man who brought him here. Delos. He didn't like the man. He thought Delos was little more than a mean man, the kind his mother warned him to stay away from.

~ * ~

For three days, Peter sulked, only leaving his bunk for the two meals they were allotted each day. He hated the food, but when he complained, Mrs. Henderson administered a punishment he knew he'd never forget.

In all his life, he'd known nothing but love and affection. If he were punished, it would be by sitting in the naughty chair at the daycare center while he thought over what he'd done wrong.

What had he done wrong to receive a paddling from Mrs. Henderson? He'd merely wanted his mother, to say nothing of the food she prepared for him. He wondered how Christopher and the others could be content with only two meals of the watery soup and grey oatmeal they insisted on feeding him.

"I'm sorry you got a paddling," Christopher said, sitting next to him on the bunk.

"How can you eat…?" he left the rest of this thoughts unsaid.

"You have to get used to it. I know it's hard when you remember what it was like before you came here. I've known nothing different since I was a baby when I was brought here. Think about it. Ain't never seen anyone leave until they either die or get growed up. I want to get growed up so I can leave here. I think you want the same thing. Think about it. I heard tomorrow we are going to start learning how to ride ponies. You don't want to miss that, do you?"

The thought of learning to ride a pony piqued Peter's interest. He sniffed loudly and willed his tears to stop. Christopher was right, this was his life. There was nothing a three-year-old boy could do to change it.

~ * ~

Within a year, Marco arrived at the Ranch and soon the three boys, Christopher, Peter and Marco became close friends.

When it was time for them to begin riding with the older boys at the age of six, they were all well versed in riding their ponies as well as roping. The thought of giving their ponies to younger boys in exchange for full sized horses was both exiting and sobering.

Peter enjoyed the work on the Ranch but was not as good as Marco. Christopher, on the other hand, did the work, but he hardly enjoyed it.

As they matured, Peter knew his future, as well as Marco's, lay in one of the ranches in Mexico.

He was concerned about Christopher. What would happen to him? Ranch work wasn't to his liking, neither was the carpentry Mr. Henderson insisted they all learn. It wasn't that he wasn't good at whatever it was he did, but there was no passion for either job he was assigned. He worked diligently, doing every job assigned to him to perfection. At night, when they returned to the dormitory, he would get a faraway look in his eyes, as though he sought more out of life than being a carpenter or a ranch hand.

One morning, Christopher disappeared from the ranch. Peter knew it was because Christopher had turned eighteen and the state would no longer send money for his care. He also knew that within another month, it would be his eighteenth birthday and he too would be moving on to one of the adventures they'd so often talked about.

It was a hot morning when Mrs. Henderson took him aside to say today was his birthday and he needed to leave the ranch. There was no time to say good-bye to anyone, even Marco.

For the first time since arriving at the ranch, Peter was allowed to leave. It was Mr. Henderson who took him into town and gave him a hundred dollars. He had no idea if that was a lot of money or what it would buy.

Standing alone on the sidewalk, he watched the hovercraft Mr. Henderson had brought him to town in disappear into the sky. Before he could decide what to do, an older man who identified himself as Pops came up to him.

"You one of them boys from out at Henderson's place?" he asked.

"Yes sir," Peter answered, unsure of what else to say. "Today is my birthday. Mrs. Henderson told me I'm eighteen now and the state won't pay for me anymore."

"I bet that old bastard gave you a hundred dollars. That won't buy you much. I'll send Ma a message and you can come home with me. I have some connections. If you've grown up out at Henderson's it's possible you know ranching and carpentry. Not much call for either of those jobs around here, but I know a rancher, Carlos. He's got a ranch just south of Mexico City. He tells me he has trouble getting good hands. I think it would be perfect for you. How well do you speak Spanish?"

"Well enough, but I do have a translator chip so I can get by."

"That sounds good. After supper tonight I'll contact him. You could be working for him by nightfall tomorrow night."

Peter was surprised by the offer, but he knew his life was turning around for the best. He'd always dreamed of a good job on one of the ranches Mr. Henderson had talked about in Mexico.

It was only a short walk to the home of Pops and Ma. From the far reaches of his memory, he equated it with the apartment he dreamed about sharing with his mother.

Pops told him to put the money from Mr. Henderson in the dresser drawer and get cleaned up for supper. Peter was amazed at the bathroom. In all his time at the ranch, his bathroom had been an outhouse and bathing had been done in a tub in Mrs. Henderson's kitchen.

Pops instructed him how to use the toilet and to flush away the waste. He then showed him the shower and explained how to use it. The luxury of this modern convenience impressed him greatly.

The meal Ma prepared them was another reminder of his life with his mother. He knew his memories were only dreams, but still he savored the food that was so alien to him.

As soon as they finished eating, he could hardly stay awake. Even when he'd worked for a full day, he'd never felt so tired. Maybe it was because he'd enjoyed a leisurely hot shower and eaten a healthy meal with real meat. At least he thought it was real meat. Whatever it was, it certainly tasted good and filled his belly more than it had been at any time in the past.

~ * ~

Out of habit, Peter awoke the next morning as soon as the sun rose on the eastern horizon. After dressing, he left the room where he'd spent the night.

To his surprise, Pops was waiting for him. "Did you sleep well?"

"I think that's the best night's sleep I've had in a long time."

"That's good because after you went to bed, I contacted Carlos. He's anxious to meet you. He says he's running short handed and is excited about getting an experienced hand. As soon as we finish breakfast, we'll be leaving. I hope you like pancakes and bacon. Ma's been busy getting everything ready for us."

Peter had no idea what pancakes and bacon were, but it had to be better than the grey oatmeal he'd eaten during the fifteen years he'd been at Henderson Ranch.

"I don't have any clothes other than the ones I'm wearing, and the spares Mrs. Henderson sent with me."

"You won't need them. Carlos takes care of everything for his hands. Now hurry up. Ma gets right feisty when folks aren't at the table on time and her food gets cold."

Peter sat in the same place he'd occupied the night before and was shocked to see the plate of food Ma put in front of him. The round things Pops called pancakes where swimming in butter and something Ma called syrup. The sweet taste was in direct contrast to the saltiness of the strips of meat he was told was bacon. To be truthful, he thought if he died today, he would die happy and well fed.

As soon as breakfast was finished, he bid Ma goodbye and promised to do his best for Señor Alfanso.

He marveled as Pops' hovercraft flew through the morning light heading south. From the height of the craft, he was able to see cities as well as what Pops called ancient ruins.

"I never thought such things existed."

"There's a whole world out there for you to see," Pops assured him.

As they continued their flight, Peter thought about the money Mr. Henderson gave him the morning before. "My money," he said, a hint of panic in his voice. "I forget to take my money."

"Don't worry about it. I'll let Ma know to look for it and send it to you. For now, you won't be needing it."

Peter took Pops at his word but still continued to think of the money he'd put in the dresser drawer the night before. In his haste to pack, he'd given it no thought, but he was certain the money was gone when he took his clothes out of the drawer. How could money just disappear?

Before he could think on it further, Pops started his descent onto the Alfanso Ranch property. Once they docked, everything happened so quickly, Peter could hardly put it into perspective.

Señor Alfanso was an impressive-looking man. His dark skin reminded Peter of his friend Marco, but rather than kind eyes, this man's eyes were menacing.

"Drop your pants," he ordered.

Peter was so frightened he did exactly as he was told. To his horror, the man fondled his private parts.

"He's well hung. If he does as he's told, he could earn the privilege of breeding one of the whores for Madam Consuelo. She says breeding them keeps them in line."

The word whore resonated within the confines of his mind. He'd been told his mother was a dirty whore. From what Mr. Henderson told him, he knew what men did to whores and he wanted no part of it.

By the time he pulled up his pants, an ankle monitor had been placed on his right foot. There was also a collar attached around his neck. A shock that went through his body told him this was something that was used to control him.

"You are my slave now," Señor Alfanso growled. "Do as you're told, and you will avoid punishment. For now, you will be taken to isolation, so I know you aren't carrying some gringo disease."

Peter refused to say anything. In his brief moment of freedom, he'd traded one nightmare for another.

From behind him, Peter could hear what could only be called a sizzle. When he turned to see what was making the noise, he saw a man he didn't recognize carrying what looked like a small branding iron. He sniffed the air but couldn't smell any smoke from a fire that would be used to heat the iron. It terrified him just the same.

Señor Alfanso ripped off Peter's shirt and pressed the implement against the skin of his upper left arm. The pain was instant and the smell of burning skin turned his stomach.

"What did you do to me?" he managed to ask, despite the pain.

"I told you, you are mine, bought and paid for. I brand what is mine. Be glad this is a laser branding iron and not the white-hot ones used on the animals. If you ever decide to try and run away, everyone will know you belong to the A BAR A ranch."

The isolation Señor Alfanso spoke of was a stark room, with a single bunk. Once the door closed, he heard the lock click into place. There was a high window with bars on it. Even if he could have reached it, there was no way he could have ever escaped. Before studying the room further, he stumbled to the bunk and collapsed, being careful not to lay on his left side. Despite the pain, he fell into a troubled sleep.

When he awoke, the pain had subsided enough for him to take a more complete inventory of the cell in which he'd been imprisoned. At the bottom on the door was a rectangular slot. It wasn't until evening when he knew what the opening was for. A bowl of food that looked little better than what he'd eaten at Henderson Ranch, was pushed into the room. Realizing his breakfast had been several hours earlier, he picked it up and hungrily ate everything he'd been given.

As evening fell, he made his way to the bunk and hunkered down for the night. There was a little light from the moon shining through the barred window, but it wasn't enough to see much of anything other than the darkness that encompassed the entire room.

~ * ~

By morning, the reality of his situation finally set in. It was as though he was reliving the first days when he was taken to Henderson Ranch all over again. In his realization, he remembered the exercises Mr. Henderson insisted the boys do at least two to three mornings a week.

While the other boys grumbled about the mandatory exercises, Peter enjoyed them. He made it a point to do them each morning before the others awoke to begin their day. He decided the hard work he did exercising not only built up his muscles, but also his stamina. Between the exercise and the ranch work, he trained his body to be able to exist on the meager food they were served.

This new chapter in his life was no different than the one he'd left behind. While in isolation, he would, once again, begin his regiment of exercise. With no work to do, he ate everything he was given, in the hopes of becoming accustomed to the food.

By the end of his isolation, he could feel his muscles building and his strength getting back to what it had been at Henderson Ranch.

After two weeks of seeing no one, the overseer finally came to release him and give him his work assignment.

"So, you're the new one," the man said as he stepped into the cell that had been his prison. "You're not what I expected."

"I'm sure I'm not. Since you can see I have no terrible disease, what will I be doing?"

"Not so fast. From the information the boss gave me, you're eighteen years old. To him you're number 596. I want to know your name."

"It's Peter."

"Peter what? You have to have a last name."

Over the years, since his father had kidnapped him and allowed Delos to take him to Henderson Ranch, every morning while he exercised, he repeated his last name and his mother's name. She had been Rita Simes and he was Peter Simes.

"It's Simes," he replied. "It's been a long time before anyone but me has said it, though. It's not important. At least that's what Mr. Henderson told me."

"We've bought slaves from Henderson before, and none of them are built like you. If you're from that place, why aren't you scrawny like the rest of them?"

"That's for me to know and you to find out. Now what will I be doing? This sitting around is getting old real fast."

"Today you ride with me. I'll evaluate your riding and roping skills. We've got calves to brand. I hope you aren't squeamish when it comes to things like that."

Peter shrugged his shoulders. "Been doin' it since I was six years old. I think I can handle it."

The overseer led him out of the cramped room and into the bright morning sunlight. Before doing anything else, he was led to a shower room and told to take off his clothes and clean himself. He expected to feel needles of cold water. Instead, the water was warm, but not hot. The soap was the same harsh lye soap he'd used all his life. It felt good to wash the grime from the isolation room, combined with the sweat from his morning exercises, from his body.

As soon as he was dry, he was given a pair of jeans, a shirt that buttoned down the front, a pair of socks, a pair of boots and a hat. It surprised him to realize these were new clothes. All of the clothes he wore at Henderson Ranch were those that others had either outgrown or left behind when they aged out.

"You be sure to take care of them clothes, boy. At the bunkhouse, there is another set. They have to last you for a year. If they get ripped or ruined, you might have to do your work buck naked. 'Course, there are some hands who wouldn't mind that one bit. They don't have a hankerin' for gals, if you get my drift."

"I get your drift. So, what do I call you other than overseer?"

The man seemed to be surprised at Peter's straightforward attitude as well as the questions he knew slaves weren't supposed to ask.

"You remind me of myself when I first came here. I've worked my way up to this position. You can call me Hank."

Peter nodded. He doubted he would ever use the man's given name, it wouldn't be seemly, but it was important information.

~ * ~

After a day in the saddle, Peter believed he'd proven his worth. It came as a shock when he was taken to the bunkhouse after an unsatisfying evening meal. Instead of being shown to a bunk, he was told to climb to the top of one of the sets of bunk beds and he was then shackled, hand and foot, to the metal of the frame to the bed.

"What if I have to relieve myself during the night?" he asked.

Hank laughed. "You'll have to piss yourself. Just remember that mattress ain't very thick and there's someone else sleeping below you. You piss all over them and they won't be none too happy with you."

Peter didn't even try to pull at his shackles. He realized they were there to restrain him and take away any freedom he might have had. Being shackled to the bed throughout the night meant he would be unable to continue his early morning exercise routine. Without that, how would he ever be able to survive on the Alfanso Ranch?

~ * ~

Days turned into weeks, weeks into months, and soon he'd been enslaved for almost two years. On the anniversary of his enslavement, he'd been given two new sets of clothing to replace the old ones that had become little more than rags after wearing them day in and day out for the entire year.

Although he managed to do his work, without his exercise routine, he could feel his strength and stamina waning. He'd also noticed that the meager meals seemed to be more watered down the longer he was there.

Over his time there, he'd often been offered one of the girls from the whorehouse Señor Alfanso mentioned when he first arrived. Each time he refused to use one of the women who was offered to him, he'd been punished.

Punishments ranged from being locked in the isolation room for several days to being publicly whipped for his refusal of what Hank and Señor Alfanso considered to be a privilege. To Peter, it was better to take the beatings than to have anything to do with a dirty whore. All his life, he'd been told how is mother was a dirty whore, therefore he equated the girls with the mother he hardly remembered. It had been years since he could even visualize what her face once looked like.

~ * ~

It had been a particular hard day of riding, roping and branding the new calves, leaving Peter feeling the effects of no daily exercise combined with the watered-down rations, as he called the meals he was given.

As he rode into the yard, he realized something was amiss. Several strange hovercrafts were docked, and some extremely tall men were putting security cuffs on both Señor Alfanso and Hank.

As soon as he and the other slaves dismounted, one of the strangers approached them. "We have come to free you," he said.

Many of the slaves, including Peter, began to cry. The last time he thought of freedom was when he had been taken to Pops' home. There for one night, he'd been free. Mr. Henderson didn't dictate what he was to do each day, he was given good food to eat, and he'd slept in a soft bed. One he'd been sold to Señor Alfanso, he thought he would never again know such freedom in this lifetime.

Overwhelmed by emotion, he fell to his knees. To his surprise, the stranger standing closest to him, helped him to his feet.

"My name is Radon. I am from the Alien complex outside of Mexico City. For the past few months, we have been investigating the trafficking of slaves between the United States and Mexico. There have been several raids made upon these ranches and there will be more to come. I have been assigned as your mentor. As soon as we remove your ankle bracelet and shock collar, we will be taking you to our complex for medical treatment and a complete evaluation. Throughout this process, I will be your mentor. Your wellbeing is of our upmost importance."

Although Peter heard what Radon was telling him, he had a hard time comprehending the meaning of it all. His body craved the exercise and nutrition he needed, and his thirst was far worse than he ever remembered it being. The allotted portion of water had been consumed early in the day as the temperature had risen drastically. He heard someone say it wasn't a fit day for man or beast to be outside.

Radon had been horrified when he first saw the slaves riding in from their day's work. With the temperatures reaching almost one hundred and twenty degrees, he'd expected to find them confined to the bunkhouse. Instead, when they arrived, they were greeted only by Señor Alfanso, the overseer, Hank, and two barking guard dogs. It was evident the dogs were trained to subdue or kill on demand.

Before the dogs could attack, one of his companions had set up a force field around them that would keep the dogs at bay while they carried out their assignment.

Now, as he held this young man in his arms, he realized the boy was little more than a living breathing skeleton. Around him, his companions ministered to the other slaves they were freeing. It was beyond him how any of them had been able to survive in this heat, to say nothing of doing hard physical labor.

Standing up, Radon cradled his charge in his arms, as though he was a newborn baby. He knew the boy would need medical assistance and he was thankful the complex was just a short flight away. Not only his charge, but many of the others, were in dire need of medical attention.

"You can't take them away from me," Señor Alfanso protested. "They are mine, bought and paid for. How do you expect me to run my ranch?"

"We don't," Radon's superior, Playnor, said. "Your ranch, as well as all of the livestock and any other assets we find are being turned over to the Mexican government. As for you, we will be detaining you until such time as your trial is scheduled."

"You-you can't," Señor Alfanso declared. "Tell them, Hank, we are free men. We've done no wrong."

"Hand me two of those shock collars," Playnor demanded.

Radon was the first to offer the collar he'd released from Peter's neck. From the look in Playnor's eyes, he knew the two prisoners would soon be on the receiving end of the punishment they'd doled out to these slaves over the years.

While Radon and three of his companions boarded the first hovercraft to take off with their charges, he could hear the screams of the prisoners as the shock collars delivered electric shocks through their bodies. He wished the young men they'd rescued were able to hear the torment of their oppressors, but it was evident all of them had lost consciousness.

Even though he hadn't heard the pilot alert the complex as to the condition of their passengers, he knew they would be met by the complex's medical team. The team worked quickly, transferring the young men to gurneys and starting IV fluids.

Unwilling to let this young man out of his sight, he walked beside the attendant taking the boy to the intensive care unit of the hospital. He needed to be able to put a name to his charge and check it against any computer files he could find on missing persons. As horrific as this assignment had been, the thought of reuniting someone with people who were looking for them was satisfying.

~ * ~

While the myriad of medical exams was being done, Radon's charge had been put into an induced coma. Through his IV, he'd been given much needed fluids and the nutrients his body craved.

"How is he doing this morning?" Radon asked the attending doctor.

"He's much better. We are planning to reverse the coma this morning. Don't expect him to be too coherent, at least not at first. He'll be confused for at least the first twenty-four hours. After that I'm certain he'll be able to answer all of your questions."

Radon nodded. It was what he expected. Before he trained for his current position, he'd done the preliminary studies to become a physician. One semester in the emergency room and he'd changed his major to become a security agent. In other words, he knew enough about medicine to know the dangers, though was unable to act on his knowledge.

As soon as the doctor completed his physical examination, he administered the drug to reverse the coma. Radon found himself holding his breath as he saw eye movement behind the boy's closed lids. This was the first indication of consciousness returning to his body for the first time since he collapsed at the ranch, days earlier.

Moments later, the boy's eyes opened, and, for the first time, he stared into expressive green eyes. At the ranch he'd taken no notice of eye color. He'd had too many other concerns at that time. Physical condition outweighed physical characteristics during those first few moments of contact.

"Wh-where am I?" The boy's words were whispered and almost inaudible.

"For now, all you need to know is that you are free and safe," Radon assured him.

He stepped back, allowing the doctor to explain everything that was being done to and for the patient.

"Can you tell us your name?" Radon heard the doctor ask.

For a moment, the boy gave them a blank stare. Within the space of only a minute, a light of intelligence shone in his eyes. "Peter, Peter Simes."

Radon took note of the name so he could research it once he had access to the main computer for the complex. For now, he typed the name into his communicator. By the time he returned to the security office, he should have a printout of any information generated by the name.

Peter tried to sit up, but the doctor forced him to continue to lay flat. "Who is that other man?" he asked. "I recognize his voice."

The fact Peter wanted to know his identity was a positive in Radon's book. He took a step closer to the bed, to position himself into Peter's line of vision.

"I'm certain you don't remember, but my name is Radon. I was a member of the team sent to rescue all of the slaves from the Alfanso Ranch. I have been assigned as your mentor."

"You said I am free, am I really free? I thought I was free when I met Pops, but he sold me to Señor Alfanso."

"I assure you the nightmare is over. It all came to light several months ago, but we can talk about that later. For now, you need to rest."

Peter nodded and allowed his eyes to close as he drifted off to a natural sleep.

He needs to rest, and I have more information to research, Radon thought to himself. For some reason, the name Pops had come up in one of the briefings. He needed to know what connection the man had to Peter. It was a mystery and one that was unraveling with every small bit of information he was able to glean.

As soon as he knew Peter was asleep, Radon made his way to his office. There he met with Playnor and several other mentors.

"How is your charge doing?" Playnor asked.

"He's awake. I now have his name as well as the name of someone he seems to be afraid of."

Playnor's face lit up. "Tell us what you've learned."

"My charge was able to tell us his name is Peter Simes. When I told him he was free, he mentioned someone named Pops. For some reason, I feel like I've heard that name before, maybe in one of the briefings."

"I've got it," one of the other mentors said. "I'm making a printout for each of us. We should have all the answers we need in the next few minutes."

Radon sat down at the desk and looked at the papers in his hand. The first sheet had the header of Peter Simes.

Peter Simes was reported to have been kidnapped by his biological father, Drake Nivens, seventeen years ago, from his biological mother in St. Joseph, Missouri.

The next page carried the heading of Drake Nivens.

There are arrest warrants issued for Drake Nevins in Missouri for kidnapping and in Montana for the first-degree murder of Delos Reynolds, the same year as the kidnapping.

"This guy is one bad character," Radon said, hardly knowing he'd put voice to his thoughts.

"Not only that," one of his colleagues commented. "I've been reading about Pops. His real name is Paul Grainger, and his wife is Doreen. They are going on trial next week in conjunction with that raid on Henderson Ranch a few months ago. Is it possible that was where Peter grew up?"

It all made sense. Why else would Peter mention Pops? "I have a feeling Peter needs to be at that trial. He's not strong enough to be able to testify, but he needs the satisfaction of seeing justice done. It's too bad the Henderson trial is completed. If I'm right, he suffered as much at the hands of those monsters as he did on the Alfanso Ranch. I can't even begin to envision what all of those boys went through."

Chapter Three

Peter could hardly believe the information he'd been given about not only Pops and Ma, but also his biological parents. The very thought he'd been kidnapped by his father and the same man was wanted for murder in Montana made him want to vomit.

The information on his biological mother was equally disturbing. Ever since he arrived at Henderson Ranch, he'd been told she was a dirty whore, when in reality she was a medical secretary.

His entire life had been a lie.

"Can I go to the trial for Pops and Ma?" he asked Radon.

"That's what we've been discussing. We all agree you need to be at the trial, but your doctor doesn't think you are strong enough to testify."

"Are they certain they have enough evidence to convict them?"

Radon stood quietly by his bed for a moment. "That's the reason we feel it is necessary for you to be there. Even if you don't testify, you will give credence to the evidence that will be presented to the court."

Peter agreed. He knew he wasn't strong enough to testify at such an important trial. Even so, he did want to be there to see justice done.

~ * ~

The day before the trial, Peter and Radon flew to the town in Nevada where the trial for the Grainger's was being held.

Even taking the flight exhausted Peter. He wondered how he would react to witness the trial scheduled to begin the next morning.

"I hope I'm up to this," Peter said, once they checked into their hotel.

"Just remember you don't have to testify, only observe. I have a feeling your presence in the courtroom will have more of an impact than any testimony you would ever give. For now, my friend, I suggest you rest."

Peter agreed. Although, when he closed his eyes and laid back on the bed, his mind remained active. Over and over again he replayed the afternoon and evening he'd spent in the home of Pops and Ma. At the time he'd looked at them as his saviors, when in reality they had betrayed him in the same way as his biological father.

In his musings, he thought about what he'd read concerning his father. The paper said he was wanted for the first-degree murder of Delos Reynolds. When he'd first read over the information, he hadn't given it much thought. Now the name Delos suddenly meant something to him.

Delos was the name of the man who took him to Henderson Ranch. Even though he'd only been three years old, he remembered that day vividly. After going with his father, he was afraid of the man called Delos. If his own father could slap him, what could this big man do? He remembered Mr. Henderson giving the man money before taking Peter to the dormitory.

Knowing that his father was accused of killing Delos, he was certain he'd been sold to Mr. Henderson and his father didn't want to split the money with his partner.

"What chance do I have in this world with a murderer for my father?"

Radon was immediately at his bedside. "No matter what your father is or was, it has no reflection on you. Your only connection with the man was at the moment of conception and the few hours you were with him when he kidnapped you. That is not enough time for him to make a lasting impression on you. Don't worry about that now. The doctor said I should give you this medication so you can get some rest. Tomorrow will be a trying day."

~ * ~

The courtroom was intimidating for Peter. There were many young men he recognized from Henderson Ranch. Most of them were older than himself. Men who as boys had disappeared from the ranch when they reached their eighteenth birthdays. To his surprise, he recognized Christopher, his first friend at the ranch.

"Christopher, is that you?" Peter asked.

"It's Chris now," he replied, a light of recognition showing in his eyes. "Where have you been since you left the ranch?"

"After I left the ranch, Mr. Henderson gave me a hundred dollars and took me into town. Before I knew it, Pops came up to me and took me home with him. I thought the nightmare was over, but it was only just beginning. The next morning, Pops took me to a ranch in Mexico. When we arrived, the rancher came and put shackles on my ankles and a shock collar around my neck. He paid Pops some money and took me with him. If you thought the Hendersons' ranch was bad, it was nothing compared to the one in Mexico. We were chained to our beds at night so we wouldn't run away, and the overseers made certain we did our work during the day. You know how I used to exercise in the early mornings? Well, I couldn't do that because of being chained to the bed.

"I couldn't believe it when they raided the ranch and took us to the Alien complex just outside of Mexico City. When they told me that it was all because of you, I couldn't believe it. I don't know how I could ever repay you."

"There's no repayment needed. Are they treating you well at the complex?"

"I've only been there for about a week, but they have been giving me good medical treatment, the best food I've ever eaten, and they tell me they're going to give me the education I was denied as a child."

"That's good. They're doing the same for me and for Marco, although now he's called Mark. I've actually found both sides of my family and the people on my mother's side are buying the ranch. They want to turn it into a school for the children who were taken from there and they want Mark to manage it for them."

"What happened to the Hendersons?"

Peter watched as Chris swallowed down what he decided must be gall that came into his throat at the mention of their former captors. "They were tried in this very courthouse and sentenced to life imprisonment in a penal colony on the dark side of the moon."

Hearing those words brought immediate satisfaction. Chris assured Peter that never again would the Hendersons be able to harm any more children.

Their conversation came to an end when Paul and Doreen Granger were brought into the courtroom. They each wore a nondescript orange jumpsuit with shackles on their ankles and hands.

"All rise," the bailiff announced. "This court is now in session. The Honorable Phillip Armstrong presiding."

Although it was still hard to stand for any length of time, Peter joined Chris and got to his feet. He was pleased to have Radon at his side so he would be able to stand until they were instructed to return to their seats. If nothing else had been learned at Henderson Ranch, it was obedience.

The prosecution presented their case and called several young men to the stand. Each of them told the same story as Peter had told Chris earlier.

At last, it was Chris' turn to take the stand. Peter knew whatever Chris said, he was making a case against Pops and Ma. He prayed his friend would be able to state, not only his own case, but Peter's too.

"Please state your name," the prosecutor ordered.

"Christopher Laughlin," he replied.

"How do you know the defendants, Paul and Doreen Granger?"

Chris related the way Paul, a.k.a. Pops, had approached him on the street and insisted he come to their home. When he mentioned Patrick Ernst, Pops had been able to contact the man almost immediately.

"How did you hear about Patrick Ernst?"

"My friend, Mark, said he'd heard about how Patrick was giving men like me a place to stay. I learned later that Mr. Henderson told Mark to tell me that. I wasn't any good at ranching, and he thought if I were sent to Ernst's group, I would, more than likely, be killed because of my mixed blood. I was lucky that they never found out about my heritage until we made the raid on the complex of the Aliens in Denver. Once I told them of my background, I knew I would no longer be welcomed in their group. I was blessed when the Aliens allowed me to stay and receive the education that I'd been denied at Henderson Ranch."

"How were you treated in the Granger home?" the defense attorney asked in his cross examination.

"For the first time, I had a good meal and a soft bed."

"If they treated you so well, why are you testifying against them?"

"When I went there, I had a hundred dollars that Mr. Henderson had given me. When I left, I no longer had the money. I didn't see the money change hands, but I heard enough while I was with Petrik's group to understand that he paid people like the Grangers to supply him with recruits for his militant group. At one time, Patrick told me I was his, bought and paid for. It wasn't the torture that the guys who were sent to Mexico endured, but it was bad enough."

"Bad enough how?" the defense attorney pressed.

Chris continued to tell of the living conditions as well as the poor food they were given while living with the skinheads.

It was almost noon when Chris finished his testimony and the court recessed for the midday meal.

Peter watched as Chris was met by an alien, who was probably his mentor from the Denver complex.

~ * ~

The afternoon session was about to be called to order when the Grangers were brought back into the courtroom. Peter could tell Chris was as shocked by what he saw as he was.

Doreen Granger, who had walked in with her head held high just hours earlier, now leaned heavily on a cane. It was also evident she was wearing heavy makeup that made her look much older than she had for the morning session.

The first person called to the stand was Doreen.

"Mrs. Granger, were you and your husband collaborating with Theodore Henderson to sell the boys from Henderson Ranch to groups like the Mexican ranchers and Patrick Ernst?"

Her reply was hardly more than a harsh whisper. "Paul would often bring home young men he met on the street. He called it his Christian mission in life. I would give them a good meal, a hot bath and a clean bed. Once they left, I had no idea where they went or what happened to them."

From the first row of the courthouse, there was an audible gasp.

"She's lying," Peter whispered to Radon, knowing full well Chris was voicing the same opinion to his mentor.

Peter watched as Radon and the man Chris introduced as Cassion, exchanged knowing glances. It was evident they were both thinking the same thing.

"I know," Cassion said. "Before we took our seats, I talked to the prosecuting attorney. It's something we were expecting."

Peter watched as Chris took a cleansing breath before looking to his left at Peter and the other young men who had testified earlier in the day. It was evident he and Chris weren't the only ones feeling the effects of Doreen's lies.

Rather than concentrate on his internal thoughts, Peter turned his mind to the cross examination of Doreen.

"You say you had no idea of what happened to the young men after they left your home, but the testimony this morning tends to tell a different story. What do you have to say about that?"

Doreen licked her lips and stared directly at the men in the front row who had been called to the stand earlier in the day.

"You know how young men like to embellish stories. It's not my fault they are all ignorant in the ways of the world. They like to make things look like something they aren't. We did nothing but give them a place to stay when they seemed to be lost and alone."

"Each of the men said they were given money when they left the Henderson Ranch. They also said when they left your home the money was missing. Do you have any idea what happened to their money?"

"What do those bastards know about money? They probably squandered it long before they ever arrived at our house. They were nothing more than ignorant misfits. You can't give money to stupid people and hope to have them know what to do with it."

Peter couldn't believe what he was hearing. He remembered the money he had when he arrived at the Granger home. Thinking back on it, he recalled putting the stash of five twenty-dollar bills into the dresser drawer when he went to bed for the night. He'd been so tired, and the bed was so soft, it was possible someone could have come into the room and taken the money while he slept.

Tears of grief flowed down his cheeks. He wasn't ashamed of them. Instead, his shame was reserved for the two people who had treated him with respect for the first time in his life. They were no better than Mr. and Mrs. Henderson. They just disguised their motives. Not only did they steal the money he'd been given, but they had sold him, as well as many others, into lives that were not much different from how they'd been treated throughout their childhood.

Doreen left the stand and leaned heavily on her attorney as he helped her to go back to the seat where she'd sat for the entire morning.

Peter could feel no sympathy for the woman who looked more like a frail little grandmother than someone who had lied under oath and stolen the future for so many of the young men who left Henderson Ranch.

Paul Granger, although not as frail looking as his wife, came across as being innocent of conspiring with Theodore Henderson and accused the earlier witnesses of lying about what had transpired after they left the Henderson Ranch. Like his wife before him, he painted a picture of someone who only wanted to help those he thought were inferior to himself and his wife.

"I can't take much more of this," Peter heard Chris say.

In response, Peter watched as Cassion put his hand on Chris' knee. "Don't be too hasty. Granger is digging his own grave with every lie he tells. When I talked to the prosecutor, he assured me that when the cross examination begins, he will be presenting the bank records for both Paul and Doreen Granger. I think you'll be surprised when you see what they reveal."

Before the cross examination could begin, the judge called a recess for the day. From the expression on Paul's face, it was evident he was relieved not to have to answer any more questions for the day. Perhaps the man was thinking he'd made a mistake in agreeing to take the stand in his own defense.

"They put on quite a show, didn't they?" Cassion asked as they left the courthouse. "Thank goodness the jury didn't believe a word of what they said."

His comment caught Peter completely off guard. "How can you say that? They made it sound like we were the liars, and they were clean as the freshly fallen snow."

"You concentrated too much on the lies they were telling. I, on the other hand, watched the faces of the jury. They were disgusted by every lie that came out of both of the defendant's mouths. It's evident they know the difference between the truth and a lie. Tomorrow will be the turning point in this trial."

Peter and Radon were going into the dining room of their hotel when they met Cassion.

"Are you staying at this hotel?" Chris' mentor asked.

"Yes, we are," Radon replied. "Peter was hoping he could have a chance to talk to Chris."

"I think that can be arranged. I was just getting ready to order dinner for Chris so he could eat in his room. It's been a trying day. Order whatever you want, then you can join him for dinner."

They waited for their order to be filled before taking the elevator to the floor where Chris's room was located. Chris answered the door almost as soon as Cassion knocked.

"I met Peter when he was going into the dining room. He was looking for you and I thought the two of you might enjoy sharing the evening meal. I will be eating with my contemporaries from Mexico. We all came here at the same time and rarely have an opportunity for face-to-face conversations."

Chris stepped aside so the food cart could be wheeled into the room. Once Cassion left, Chris turned his attention to Peter.

"Are you as hungry as I am?" he asked Peter.

"I didn't think I was, but my mentor insisted I needed to eat. Now that I smell the food, I realize how hungry I actually am. I didn't eat much at the midday meal. I guess it was because of nerves or it could be the fact I was used to not eating three meals a day when I worked on the ranch."

Chris nodded and started taking the covers from the dishes that contained their meal. Each plate was loaded with steaming roast beef, mashed potatoes drowning in rich beef gravy, and green beans. Other bowls on the cart contained a green salad with a light Italian dressing, as well as a piece of apple pie. Chilled bottles of water were also on the cart.

"It looks like a feast fit for a king," Chris observed.

Peter waited until Chris started to eat before tentatively following his lead. "I'm still learning how civilized people eat. You know, with real silverware and not slop you can almost drink out of the bowl."

"What was it like on the ranch?" Chris finally asked.

"Maybe I should start with leaving Henderson Ranch. Old man Henderson no more than left me off on the street of that town, when Pops approached me. He took me back to his house and got me some clean clothes. He suggested I put the hundred dollars Henderson gave me in the top dresser drawer for safe keeping."

Chris nodded. "It was the same with me."

"That evening, Ma served us the evening meal. As I recall, she put the food on the plates before she gave it to us. I remember I was hardly able to keep my eyes open after we ate, so I went right to bed. The more I think about it, the more convinced I am that the food was drugged."

"Drugged?" Chris questioned. "I never thought about that, but I think you might be onto something. I remember going to bed almost as soon as we finished eating that night, as well as the other nights I was there. You might be on to something, but of course, we could never prove it."

"I agree, but it's the only reason I think that's what happened. I've always been a light sleeper but that night I don't recall anything after I went to bed, until Pops woke me up the next morning. That was when he said he'd found me work on a ranch in Mexico. He said the pay was good and since I knew a little Spanish I could do well working there, especially with the translator chip. While I took a shower, Ma fixed us something to eat. I have to admit it was the best food I'd ever eaten, until I was rescued and taken to the Alien complex. I'm sure my mother made good food, but I was too young to remember it."

"I felt the same way. I thought I'd never be hungry again until I got mixed up with Ernst and his group. The food was a little better than what we got at the ranch, but not by much."

Peter took another bite of his food before he began to speak again. "As soon as we finished eating, Pops and I got into his hovercraft and flew it down to the ranch in Mexico. As soon as we arrived, we were met by Señor Alfonso. He handed Pops some money and put an ankle bracelet on my right leg. He told me I was his, bought and paid for. From that moment on, my every move was monitored. For the first two weeks I was there, I was put into isolation. I was free to move around the room, so I continued to do my exercise routine. Once I came out of isolation, I was to work from six in the morning until eight in the evening, in the barns, as well as helping with the branding. There were only two meals a day and they were less than satisfactory."

"When did you realize that the money Henderson gave you was gone?" Chris asked.

"We were on the way to Mexico, I told Pops I'd forgotten to take it with me. He said he'd have Ma look for it and send it to me. Of course, no money ever arrived. I'm certain they took it."

"I'm afraid you're right. Cassion told me the prosecution is looking into their banking records. Do you remember when you were there with them?"

"It was about two months after you left. Time doesn't mean much to me, but I always counted the baths we got to take. Every time we took four baths, I knew another month had passed. It was eight baths between the time you left and the time I left."

"I forgot about the fact baths were only available to us once a week. I thought swimming in the creek during the summer and being able to bathe with water heated on the stove twice weekly at Ernst's camp was luxury. Since coming to the complex, I enjoy taking a daily shower.

"According to the information on my DNA chip, my birthday is in June, so that means you must have left in August."

They spent the remainder of the evening talking about their experiences since they were last together on Henderson Ranch.

It was getting late when Cassion and Radon returned to the suite. "Have you two had enough time to get caught up?" Cassion asked.

"I doubt there will ever be enough time to learn everything Peter and the others have to tell me about their past," Chris replied. "Of course, we have a lifetime to get caught up. I'm certain our paths will be crossing many times in the future."

~ * ~

Court was once again in session and the defense attorney rested his case. Immediately, the prosecutor asked to call a rebuttal witness to the stand.

Peter and Chris watched as Cassion took the stand and presented the financial statements he'd obtained for both Paul and Doreen Granger.

"What did you find in these statements?" the prosecuting attorney asked.

"Into the account for Doreen Granger, there were regular deposits of one hundred dollars. They all align perfectly with when each of the boys from the ranch was dropped off close to the Granger home. Days later, Paul Granger deposited large amounts of money into his account. Had we gotten financial records for Theodor Henderson, I'm certain we would have seen similar deposits on corresponding dates to those made by Mr. Granger. These deposits into the Granger account were no longer made after Peter was taken to Mexico. We know, for certain, there were other young men who aged out of the program at the ranch after Peter did, but by that time there were no more deposits into the Grangers' accounts. It is our assumption that the Hendersons' needed additional finances."

Peter knew Chris was listening intently to Cassion's testimony. They'd been told that Chris was going to be called back to the stand. Earlier when he'd testified, he'd faced the Grangers as he remembered them. This time, he would have to face the same people, only they looked more like very elderly and sick people who didn't deserved what was happening to them.

Peter ached for his friend. He could tell that Pops and Ma were glaring at him with contempt. They were no longer the saviors they once thought them to be. With all the information they'd been given in the last few hours, they now looked more like the predators they were.

"You are still under oath," the prosecutor informed him.

Chris nodded.

"You indicated that the Grangers were good to you. Why then did you want to take the stand again?"

"My friend, Peter, and I had a long talk last night. We were each given a hundred dollars from Mr. Henderson. He told us that we were to use the money to start our new lives. Everything happened so quickly while I was with them, I didn't think about the money again until I was with Patrick's group. When I mentioned it, Patrick told me that since I was with him, I didn't need it and to forget about it."

"How long were you at the Granger home before you went with Patrick Ernst?"

"It was interesting. As soon as I mentioned I'd been told about Patrick Ernst, Pops was able to contact him. It was as though he was waiting for me to mention Ernst's name. I left three days after I arrived."

The prosecutor returned to his seat and the defense attorney got to his feet. "Are you certain you were given money when you left the Henderson Ranch?"

The question seemed to have caught Chris off guard. "How could I forget something like that? In all my life, I'd never had money. I had no idea of what it was for or how to use it. I was in awe of holding something like that in my hands."

"Are you certain you didn't take the money with you and are making all of this up to make Mr. and Mrs. Granger look guilty?"

Chris looked to be appalled by the accusation. "I was abused as a child and more so when I became an adult. It wasn't the same as the physical abuse I suffered at the hands of Mr. and Mrs. Henderson. The abuse I suffered while with Patrick Ernst was mental and emotional. Nevertheless, the one thing I was taught as a child and a young adult, was that the most important thing in life was to tell the truth, no matter what the consequences. I didn't want to believe the Grangers were part of the abuse going on at Henderson Ranch, but from everything I've learned, they are not as innocent as they want everyone to believe."

There were no more questions and with a look of relief, Chris left the stand and returned to his seat next to Cassion.

Closing arguments were made and the jury was sent back to the jury room for deliberations. For both Peter and Chris, the morning had been draining.

"Do you think I have time to go back to the suite and take a nap?" Chris asked.

Peter agreed. Even though he hadn't testified, he was exhausted.

"I think Cassion will agree with me when I suggest the two of you get something to eat instead of taking a nap. The fact neither of you ate much for breakfast didn't escape us."

Although neither of them was interested in eating, they both ordered a bowl of soup and a salad. They were just finishing their lunch when someone came from the court to tell them the jury had returned with their verdict.

"I can't believe how quickly they came to their decision," Cassion said, as they made their way back to the courthouse.

"Is that good or bad?"

"It's hard to tell. Hopefully, they saw through the façade the defense tried to show. Only time will tell."

Once inside the courthouse, Chris and Peter took their seats and were surprised to see the Grangers enter the room. Although they looked frail hours earlier, now they looked as though they were on death's door.

Everyone took their seats, and the jury handed their decision to the judge. After looking at the paper he turned his attention to the jury. "Is this your unanimous decision?"

The foreperson of the jury stood and affirmed their decision had been unanimous.

The judge instructed the Grangers to stand to hear the verdict.

"Paul and Doreen Granger, you have been found guilty of all of the charges leveled against you. At this time, this court is sentencing you to life imprisonment in the penal colony under the ice cap of Antarctica. Following these proceedings, you will be taken directly there to begin your sentence."

Almost immediately Doreen collapsed, and Paul tried to keep her from falling to the floor. As if the effort was too much for him, he relied on their attorney to help him support his wife's weight.

After Doreen was revived, Paul turned toward the people assembled to watch the proceedings. "This is your fault," he said, pointing directly at both Chris and Peter. "You'll rot in hell for what you've done to us."

Peter knew Chris wanted to reply, but Cassion stopped him. "Don't stoop to his level," Cassion whispered. "He's not worth it."

Chris nodded. Without saying a word, they watched as Paul and Doreen were led out of the courtroom by two aliens wearing the uniforms of guards from the penal colony.

"It's over," Chris said.

"For you, yes, but I still have to testify at the trial for Señor Alfonso. I wish you well, my friend. Again, thank you for saving me as well as many others from the horrors we've lived through for most of our lives. I pray we will meet again in the future."

Chapter Four

Peter reluctantly left Nevada with Radon and some of the other men who had been brought there from Mexico City. Saying goodbye to Chris again had been hard. Throughout their childhood and adolescence, they'd been close friends. What if they would never see each other again? Could he live the rest of his life without seeing his friend in his uncertain future?

While they'd talked, Mark's name came up. Chris assured Peter that Henderson Ranch had been purchased by the Native American side of his family and they were willing to hire Mark to manage it. Chris indicated they would be needing help with the everyday running of the ranch and he'd asked Peter if he would be willing to join them once they had everything up and running. He knew this was one decision he would have to think long and hard on before giving either Chris or Mark his answer.

~ * ~

Once he returned to the Mexico City complex, Peter was surprised at how quickly everything began to happen. He was given a complete physical at the hospital, before being discharged to take up residency in his own apartment.

Everything about the complex amazed him. At the hotel in Nevada, he'd been introduced to the moving room Radon called an elevator. Still, his apartment was something he'd never experienced before. To open the door, he could use either voice or handprint recognition. Off of the bedroom was the bathroom. It contained a free-standing shower, a sink and a self-flushing toilet. Even the bedroom was a wonder. Sleeping not only in a soft bed but without anyone else in the room was something he knew would be hard to get used to.

Once he was settled into his apartment he was taken to a classroom where the schooling he'd been deprived of as a child began in earnest. Hearing Chris talk about getting an education hadn't begun to cover the enormity of now learning all of the things every child was entitled to know.

He'd just finished his classes for the day when he found Radon waiting for him. "We have something we need to talk about," his mentor greeted him.

"You sound serious. Should I be worried?"

"Hardly. We have finally located your mother. It was difficult because she'd gotten married and moved to Canada. She wants to meet you. How do you feel about that?"

Peter's stomach began to churn. Even though he'd been told she was a medical secretary, he couldn't help remembering how he'd always been told she was a dirty whore. Losing that description of the woman who called herself his mother would be difficult.

"Where would this meeting take place?"

"She knows you would be more comfortable here, but she and her husband have young children. They also both have demanding jobs. Hers is in the medical community and he runs his own company. She would like to have you come to Canada."

"Would you go with me?"

"Of course, I will. There's more that you don't know about Canada. We've been doing a more complete examination of your DNA. It seems your father's name isn't Drake Nevins. According to the records we have found, he was born Quinton Solomon, Jr. His father was a multi-millionaire in Toronto, Canada. Although your father was an only child and he thought he inherited everything, we have uncovered some hidden assets. According to your grandfather's lawyer there was a second will. The first one left the bulk of the estate to your father and the second left the hidden assets to his oldest grandchild if one should exist. After forty years, if no grandchild were found, the inheritance would revert to charity.

In other words, you are a wealthy young man in your own right. Once we started the probe, the lawyer insisted your grandfather's body be exhumed and a complete autopsy performed."

Peter's interest was piqued. "Why would he want such a thing?"

"Because the man was in declining health, his son didn't want an autopsy. With the information that has come to light about your father, it is entirely possible the murder of Delos Reynolds wasn't the first one he'd committed. The autopsy was performed, and it is evident Quinton Solomon, Senior died of suffocation and not of natural causes. Now there is a warrant for your father's arrest by the province of Ontario for the murder of his father."

"How could someone kill their own father?" Peter asked, partially choking on the words.

As soon as he spoke the words, he remembered how he'd fantasized about killing his father throughout all the years he'd been at Henderson Ranch. Had it not been for his father, his life would have been much different.

"It's entirely possible your father is a sick man. At this point we don't know what name he is using. It seems to be quite easy for him to reinvent himself to suit his purposes. We are hoping he will try to contact you."

"If he does, will I be in danger?"

"Even if you are, nothing will be allowed to happen. My counterparts and I are committed to not only keeping you safe but to bringing your father to justice."

Peter felt as though he'd been given a ton of information to absorb within the confines of his mind. He wished he had someone close to his own age to confide in. "I need time to think on this. Do I have to give you my answer right now?"

"Of course, you don't. Take your time to come to a decision. Your mother has been waiting seventeen years to find you. Another few days won't make a difference, one way or the other."

Peter made his way to his apartment with more on his mind than he thought he could ever comprehend. Once he relaxed for a few minutes he turned on his communicator and placed a call to Chris.

Seeing his friend's face on the screen put his mind at ease. Once he told Chris everything he'd learned today, he felt better.

"That's a lot to be told all at the same time. I do suggest you meet your mother. I know meeting both sides of my family have helped me to adjust to this new life I'm living. As for your father, I wouldn't try to find him if I were you. It's entirely possible he will try to find you, especially if he gets wind of the inheritance your grandfather left you. I'm sure there's nothing they can do about the money that your grandfather left to his son, because it's more than likely gone."

"I'm grateful to you for taking my call. I honestly don't have anyone my age here to confide in."

"What about the men who were with you at the ranch?"

"I saw too many of them disappear to form friendships. Most of them were older than me and I honestly didn't trust anyone enough to get close to them. I've also been thinking about what you told me about Henderson Ranch. As many bad memories as I have about that place, it was home for most of my life. Do you think the three of us can make it into something more than what it was?"

A smile spread across Chris' face. "Between my family and Mark, they are making great plans. I also think several of the aliens from the facility here in Denver want to be included. They are great teachers and want to help as many of the men we grew up with to start new lives. We are also hoping to take in some of the younger kids that were still at the ranch when it was raided. Who knows what it will evolve into?"

"I like the sound of that. I'll talk to Radon and see if he can find some of the others who left the ranch before us."

"So, after all this talk, have you come to any decision about your mother?"

"I'm certain I'll meet with her. I'm getting stronger every day. As much as I've hated her for being a dirty whore all my life, I'm going to have to change my thinking where she is concerned. After all these years, she deserves to know what happened to me."

"Keep me posted. I know when I met both sides of my family, I was scared out of my mind. They were very accepting and both sides are anxious to be involved in any venture I decide to take on in life."

Once the connection was closed, Peter sat for a moment thinking about everything he and Chris talked about. He was surprised when the voice-activated system announced Radon was requesting admission into his apartment.

"Allow Radon admission," he said.

Silently the door slid open, and Radon entered the apartment, pushing a cart with covered dishes. "I was afraid you would not come down to the dining hall, so I ordered our meals so I could bring them up here. I know I gave you a lot to think about it and was hoping you'd like to talk about things."

Peter smiled. Other than Chris and Mark, he'd never had a friend, and even though Radon was much older, he could feel a bond forming between the two of them.

"I contacted Chris and he helped me put everything into perspective. If you know how to contact my mother, perhaps you can arrange a time when we could meet, but only if you are still willing to go with me."

Radon smiled. It was evident this was the decision he wanted Peter to make. "Of course, I will be with you. I am your mentor and ready to be of help to you whenever you need me."

Chapter Five

Rita Hodges read every article she could get her hands on about the raid on Henderson Ranch and the rescue of the children who were being raised there. She had no idea why the information was so important to her. Each news story made her wonder why it fascinated her so.

She knew the answer. Somehow, she knew the discovery of this one ranch was only the tip of the iceberg. It was entirely possible it could be the key she needed to unlock the whereabouts of the son who had been lost to her for so many years.

The automated voice of the house computer announced someone was at the door. She paid little attention, since her husband, Randy, was at home and he would see who was there.

For the third time, she watched the video of the trial for the Grangers on her communicator. As usual she scanned the faces of the young men who were in the front row of the courtroom. Could one of them be her son? Most of them looked more like walking skeletons rather than men.

Every time she watched the video, she cried tears of frustration. If this was her son's fate, it was entirely possible he had not survived to grow to adulthood.

"You have a visitor," Randy announced.

She looked up from the communicator screen to see a member of the Mounties enter her sunroom.

"I've been told you are Rita Simes."

She was shocked to hear someone call her by her maiden name. "I was Rita Simes, until I met and married my husband."

"Did you give birth to a son in 2100, by the name of Peter?"

She felt her knees go weak. Nobody, other than Randy and her daughters, knew about her background and the son she'd lost over seventeen years ago. Silently, she thanked Randy for coming to her side to support her.

"I did, but he was kidnapped by his father a long time ago. He could be dead by now for all I know."

"I assure you he is not dead. We have matched his DNA to you as well as to his father, Quinton Solomon, Jr. He was recently rescued from one of the slavery ranches in Mexico."

"You must be mistaken. My son's father was Drake Nevins."

"We have learned that was the name he was using at the time your son was kidnapped, and a man who was living with him, Delos Reynolds, was murdered. We believe he also murdered his father right here in Toronto before he changed his name. As of the moment, we have no idea what name he is using or where we can begin to look for him. Our counterparts at the Alien complexes here, in the United States, and in Mexico are helping us in our search for him."

Rita felt even weaker than she had before. With Randy's help, she slumped down into the chair she'd occupied before their visitor arrived.

"I hope I haven't distressed you too greatly, but we needed to begin with you, in order to reunite you with your son. Don't be surprised if he is reluctant to meet with you at first. It is hard telling how long he was with his father, or what has been told to him about you. Since we have ascertained he was living at both the Henderson Ranch and one of the slave ranches in Mexico, we have no idea what his mindset could be."

"I pray that Peter will want to meet me, but I will abide by his decision, no matter what it is."

"There is something else you should know. Your son is the sole heir to a hidden fortune left by Quinton Solomon, Sr. Back at the time of his death, before the turn of the century, his son claimed the inheritance he knew about and disappeared. The old man didn't trust his son and left the hidden fortune to his firstborn grandson. Once all this information came to light, the authorities had the old man's body exhumed and autopsied. It was then that we learned he was murdered, presumably by the son who disappeared after liquidating the assets he was aware of."

How could Drake be a murderer? I remember him as a caring boyfriend, until I told him about Peter. That was when he dropped out of sight. I wonder if that friend of his, Delos Reynolds, could have shed some light on his whereabouts. It's now possible, considering the man was murdered.

"When we were dating, he had a friend, Delos Reynolds. Earlier you said something about him being murdered. If you could have found him alive, you might have been able to find Drake."

"I agree with you, but from what we've learned, the body of Delos Reynolds was found almost seventeen years ago in Montana. At that time, an arrest warrant was issued for Drake Nevins, AKA Quinton Solomon, Jr., in connection with the man's murder. Our office has done a lot of research and it seems as though the man you knew as Drake is an expert on many things, to say nothing of being a murderer."

Rita felt as though she was going to be sick. She wanted this man to leave her house and take the horrible accusations about her son's father with him. She didn't want Drake to be a murderer, but it was entirely possible. If he could stoop so low as to kidnap their son, anything was possible.

~ * ~

It was two weeks before Rita heard anything more about the son who disappeared from her life when he was only three. The information came as a message on her communicator from a man by the name of Radon. It didn't take much for her to realize someone with such a name would be one of the aliens who had complexes all over the globe.

When she returned his call, she stared into the most beautiful violet eyes she'd ever seen. "I received your message, Mr. Radon," she began.

"There is no need for you to all me mister. My people go by only one name. I am contacting you as Peter's mentor. I have been caring for and guiding him since he was rescued from one of the ranches in Mexico. As such, I have informed him that you have been located and are anxious to reconnect with him. He has taken some time to make his decision and has asked me to arrange for a meeting between the two of you."

"Where is he?"

"He is being cared for and educated at our complex just outside of Mexico City. Although I know he would be more comfortable meeting you here, he has agreed to come to Canada to meet with you. He understands you have a husband and children, to say nothing of an important job. He feels it is easier for him to come to you than the other way around. Of course, I will be accompanying him to look out for his best interests. Since I am the one who worked the rescue of Peter as well as the others, I have taken on the position of mentor and friend."

Rita nodded, knowing the man could see her gesture. "Wh-when does he want this meeting to take place?"

"We are working out the logistics of such a visit. In another month, he will be having a break from his studies and would be free to travel to Canada."

"Studies?" she asked.

"Like all the boys who were raised on Henderson Ranch, he was denied a formal education. When he came to us, he could barely sign his name or do the simplest of mathematical calculations. We have been tutoring him with an accelerated teaching program and I will tell you he is highly intelligent. So far, he has surpassed all of our expectations for his progress. I've been told it is the same with his friends, Chris and Mark. It is a shame these children were taken to Henderson Ranch where they could never expect to reach their full potential."

By the time they ended the communication, a date had been set for her to be reunited with her firstborn son, Peter. Now it was up to her and Randy to tell their children of the older brother they knew existed but never thought they'd meet.

~ * ~

The next Saturday, they sat down with their daughters, twelve-year-old Peggy and ten-year-old Jenny. She was certain, after the visit from the Mounty combined with the whispered conversations between herself and Randy, they knew something was up.

"What is it, Momma?" Peggy asked.

"We have something to tell you that will change all of our lives forever," Randy replied. "We have never made a secret about your brother. He has been found and he wants to reunite with us."

It took almost an hour to tell the story, as she told it in bits and snatches between bouts of tears she couldn't control. She silently thanked Randy for helping her tell the story when she could no longer continue.

"When can we meet him?" Peggy asked, excitement flashing in her eyes.

"Like we told you, he was denied an education when he was your age, so we must wait until he has a break from his studies. According to his mentor, he will be able to come here to meet with us next month,"

Rita could tell from the change in the expression on Peggy's face that her daughter was disappointed.

"I thought maybe we could go to Mexico. We've been learning about it in school."

"Maybe someday," Randy assured her. "For now, Peter and his mentor will be coming to us. They don't want to disrupt your school schedule or our work schedule. I think he will be more comfortable getting to know us in our home rather than at the Alien complex where he is living."

Eventually, the children accepted the fact their brother was concerned for their continuity of studies. For them, it was enough they were going to get to meet someone they'd heard about all of their lives but never thought they'd meet.

Chapter Six

Peter assessed the things he'd packed for his trip to Canada. From what he'd learned, he would need warmer clothing than what was required in Mexico. Radon helped him purchase suitable pants, shirts and sweaters to prepare for the trip.

It was early in the morning when Radon came to accompany him to the docking area. "Are you ready for this adventure?" he asked.

"As ready as I'll ever be. I've researched the job my mother has and realized she wasn't a dirty whore like I was told. I never thought of her getting married or having other children, never considered having two younger sisters. I hope they don't think I'm a dummy because my level of education is not as high as theirs."

"I doubt anyone would ever think something like that. It's possible they are as exited to finally meet you as your mother is."

"I hope so. To be truthful, I have no idea how to act around girls. I've interacted with women since I arrived at the complex, but before that, I only ever knew Mrs. Henderson and Ma. All my life, I've lived among men and boys. Women, no matter what their age, frighten me more than I would like to let on."

Radon laughed at his statement. "It will take time, but you'll become more comfortable around the fairer sex. They are the glue that holds our society together. Without women, there would be no babies, men would probably screw up the entire world and…" After a short pause, he again laughed. "I guess the reason those of us of the alien race made our presence known was because a hundred years ago the world was messed up because of the men who were running things. Once you advance to start learning history, you will understand what I'm saying."

Peter smiled. He'd heard people talking about the history of the world before the aliens came to give their help and guidance. He was glad he hadn't lived during those trying times. What little he'd heard told him the twenty-second century was much more civilized.

~ * ~

"Do you think he'll like us, Mom?" Peggy asked.

"Of course, he will. You have to remember, though, he hasn't had the same kind of childhood you and your sister have enjoyed. He was only three years old when he was kidnapped. From what I've read about that terrible place where he was taken, there was no love, no care given to the boys who were raised there. Even as an adult his life has been filled with pain."

Peggy made no response. Rita knew it was because there was nothing to say. The loving child she'd given birth to and raised on her own for the first three years of his life was not the young man they would be meeting at the space port in a matter of minutes. From the pictures she'd seen, he was a handsome young man who carried the best features of both herself and Drake. What haunted her the most was the hurt she could see in his green eyes. They depicted a lifetime of hard living combined with physical, mental and possible sexual abuse at the hands of the people who raised him.

The announcement of the arrival of the hovercraft from Mexico brought all of them to attention. It was the moment they'd waited for ever since learning of Peter's existence months earlier. Even though they'd spoken via their communicators, it wasn't the same as being together face to face.

There were several other people around them, including the representatives of the law firm who handled the will for Peter's paternal grandfather, Quinton Solomon, Sr. How would her son adjust to becoming independently wealthy? Did his grandfather think that it was possible his own son would be capable of murder, therefore making a second will to see to the financial security of his grandson? There were no answers to these questions. Besides, this was neither the time nor the place for such speculations.

At the next announcement that the passengers of the hovercraft would be arriving at the waiting area, the air in the room seemed to become electrified. Although they tried to blend in with the others who were waiting for passengers, the members of the press were easy to identify. Peter was big news. Not only had he returned from over seventeen years in a living hell, he was also the grandson of one of the richest men in Canada. He was big news, and everyone was aware of it.

The door to the custom's area opened and Rita got the first glimpse of the son she hadn't seen, in person, since the day she took him to the daycare center seventeen years earlier. Even as an adult, she would have known him anywhere. The deep cleft in his chin was as striking today as it had been when he was a child. That, combined with his green eyes and shock of red hair, made her think of the little boy she'd loved and lost.

Without hesitation, she crossed the expanse between the waiting area and the doorway through which he was entering.

"Peter?" she said, her voice hardly more than a whisper. "I know you don't recognize me, but I'm your mother."

At her words, she saw tears forming in his eyes. "I dreamed of you every night, but they told me lies about you. I always wanted to go home, but…" The remainder of what he was trying to say was lost in the sobs that followed.

Here was her son, a man, not a little boy. Clinging to her as he once had when he'd been a toddler. His eyes were pleading with her to take all the hurt away, just like they had when he was three years old and skinned his knees.

~ * ~

Peter saw his mother, even before she came across the room to greet him. She was the same woman who had dominated his dreams ever since he'd been taken away by his father. He remembered the day and the promise of the adventure they were about to take.

Enfolded in her arms, he tried to tell her how much he loved and missed her, but unmanly tears cut off his words. It took several moments for him to regain his composure.

"It doesn't matter," his mother said, as she placed her hand on his cheek. "You're here and all those terrible things are behind us forever. Your step-father and sisters are anxious to meet you."

Peter shifted his gaze. Standing behind his mother were the two girls she referred to as his sisters. There was no doubt of their identities. They each carried a strong resemblance to his mother, while carrying features of the man who fathered them. He was thankful their father and his father had been two different people. In no way would he want either of them to share the shame he'd experienced after being told of his father's crimes of kidnapping and murder.

"I'm Peggy," the oldest of the girls said as she stepped forward.

He tried to read her thoughts, and realized she was looking for acceptance. Radon told him his family would probably want him to give them hugs. He'd even showed him what a proper greeting of long-lost family would be.

Tentatively, the girl held out her right hand. Rather than shaking it, as would have been customary under any other circumstances, he pulled her into a hug.

"I've never had a sister before. I hope I can live up to any expectations you have of me."

"That makes us even," Peggy assured him. "We've never had a brother before either. Guess we'll be learning what to do together. The difference is we've always known about you. Mom insisted we should celebrate your birthday every year. We also bought Christmas presents for you, just in case you would come home for Christmas. When you didn't, they were donated to a homeless shelter for women with children. When we knew you were no longer a child, we bought clothes and donated them to the needy. Now I wish we had all those presents to give you."

The tears Peter had been shedding for the first time in too many years, flowed even faster. "I don't need presents. Every gift I could ever imagine is right here. I have a family, a real family. The mother I dreamed about every night is alive. I can reach out and touch her, to say nothing of hugging her like I did when I was three years old."

Both of his sisters, as well as his mother, were crying. It was his stepfather who stepped up and shook his hand. "Welcome to our family, son. I've looked into things over the past week, and I realize it's not too late for me to adopt you, that is, if you are willing. It's my anniversary present to my wife."

Throughout the exchange with his family, Peter had forgotten about Radon being with him. To his surprise, his mentor stepped forward. "I think you have made a wise decision. Peter needs a fresh start in life and your suggestion is giving it to him. I'm certain he will be telling you of the opportunity that has been opened to him, doing something he loves, while he is here. For now, it was a long flight and I think I speak for both of us when I say we should go to the hotel to get some rest."

"Hotel?" Randy echoed. "There will be no need for such a thing. When we purchased our home, we added a guest cottage on the grounds. It was for my mother, after my father passed away. Since she is no longer with us, it has sat vacant for far too long. Ever since we knew of your arrival, Rita and the girls have been refurbishing it for you. I am hopeful you will find the accommodations to your liking."

Peter was overwhelmed. In his wildest imagination, he'd not thought about staying in such close proximity to his family.

"We need to talk to the young man."

The voice of a man standing to the far side of the terminal resonated throughout the room. It was the voice of a man who was used to being in authority. For a moment, it seemed as though he was listening to Señor Alfanso or Hank giving orders for punishment to be doled out, whether it was deserved or not.

After taking a calming breath, he turned to address the man. "What is so important that you would take me away from the family I've been deprived of for the past seventeen years?"

"We represent the estate of your late grandfather," said one of the men, who looked like a clone of the others who were with him. "I think you would like to know that you are a very wealthy man. Your grandfather provided a trust fund for you, long before you were born. At the same time, he wrote a second will leaving you with several assets he'd hidden from his son. He was one of the wealthiest men in Canada, and now you share this wealth. The fact your father is considered to be responsible for the death of his father has nothing to do with the inheritance you are entitled to."

Peter tried to comprehend what was being said. "From what I've been told, I will be in Canada for the next month. I need time with my family. If there is to be a meeting between us, it will be orchestrated by my mentor, Radon. Since I was rescued, he has been the only one who has had my best interests at heart. I am certain you understand my request. If you give your information to him, he will be in touch with you."

Without saying more, Peter turned back to his family, ignoring the lawyers who were anxious to tell him of the great wealth and prestige that awaited him in Canada. What they didn't know was that he'd already allied himself with his friends, Chris and Mark. Together they had great plans for Resurrection Ranch and the young men who would be helped by coming there.

~ * ~

Having visited both Mexico City and Carson City, Nevada, Peter had been impressed, but Toronto was something else. He never ceased being amazed by what he saw. While his mother and sisters led the way back to their home, it was Randy who insisted Peter and Radon accompany him in his personal craft.

"Rita's hovercraft is perfect for our family of four to travel comfortably, but we knew you would have luggage. Since I have the larger vehicle, I said I would bring you back with me."

"Why do you have the larger craft?" Peter asked.

"I can't lie. It's my ego. I like having a larger craft. I've always liked expensive toys. Besides, when we take family vacations, I have the room for the extra luggage and any equipment we might need. We like to go camping."

"Vacation? Camping?" Peter was confused by the terms that were unfamiliar to him.

Before Radon could answer, Randy began to explain. "You coming to Toronto from Mexico is a vacation. You are away from your home and doing something different from your daily routine. Rita, the girls and I like to go to places that are new and exciting. We've gone to the seaside, the mountains and to cities that are unfamiliar. As for camping, when we go to the mountains, or other places, we like to, 'rough' it. Sometimes, we rent a trailer where we can stay in comfort. Other times we use a tent and cook over a camp stove. It's always an adventure for all of us."

Peter nodded his head. "I've camped out many times in Mexico. I never thought of it as an adventure, though. It was just something that was expected of us when we were out working with the herd. It wasn't always possible to get back to the ranch to sleep in the bunkhouse."

"How did they keep you from running away when you weren't at the ranch proper?"

"There were always armed guards, although they wouldn't have been necessary. The shock collars we all wore were connected to the computer at the main house. If any of us ran, we could have been found within a matter of minutes. It was easier to do the work, no matter how hard and tiring it was. We all learned to endure the punishments rather than to run and possibly be beaten to death for our efforts. Call me an optimist, but I always hoped to, one day, be free."

Peter noticed a tear trickle down Randy's cheek.

"I don't know if I could have been that brave under those circumstances. Death might have been a welcome relief."

Peter understood. He knew many of his friends among the slaves had found a way to either kill themselves or provoke the guards to do it for them. He always considered it the coward's way out. In all his life, at least since his arrival at Henderson Ranch, he fought through every urge to end it all. Somehow, he knew something better was in store for him.

It amazed him how short of a trip it was to arrive at what Randy called their suburban home. Although it was in an urban area, there seemed to be a large expanse of lawn as well as a wooded area. In the distance he could see the sun sparkling off the water of a small lake. It was all very impressive to say the very least.

"I can't believe this is your home," Peter said as he took in the vista before him.

"We liked the acreage when we first looked at the house. I'd just started my business and was making good money. Added to that was an inheritance from my grandparents. If it hadn't been for that, we would have never been able to afford something this extravagant. To be truthful, I enjoy doing the yard work and the girls like playing in the woods and swimming in the lake. Of course, the first thing we did was to build the guest cottage. Unfortunately, it's sat empty for the past five years. The girls use it as a playhouse, but they've been so excited about you coming here, they insisted on helping your mother get it ready for you."

Although Peter knew the woman he'd met at the space port was his mother, he still had trouble equating the word 'Mom' with her.

He looked away from the broad expanse of lawn and saw his mother and sisters standing in front of the house. From the looks on their faces he knew they were pleased to have him with them. He wished he felt as comfortable with the situation. At the space port he'd acknowledged an immediate attraction, even a feeling of affection. Now he wasn't so certain. He knew it was because of his upbringing. Trust and affection were two things he'd been denied for most of his life.

"I will leave Peter to become better acquainted with his family," Radon said. "If you could point me in the direction of the guest house, I will take our luggage there and get settled. I am here to advise and mentor Peter, not to interfere with the reunion that is many years overdue."

As much as Peter wanted to protest, he said nothing. Ever since he'd been rescued, Radon had become his best friend. He trusted his mentor with every aspect of his life, as he knew the man had only his best interests in mind with everything he did.

Once Peter and Randy took the first steps to close the distance between his mother and sisters, he began to relax. To his surprise, it seemed as though walking to embrace his family was as natural as breathing.

~ * ~

Radon was surprised when his communicator registered a message from the lawyers who represented Peter's paternal grandfather the morning after their arrival at the Hodges' home.

"I thought I made it quite clear yesterday that it would be prudent of you to allow Peter time to adjust to finding his family."

"You did, but these holdings are vast. Time is of the essence. Should his biological father hear of this inheritance, because of the media reporting on Peter returning to Canada, he could come back to Toronto and challenge the boy's identity. It's entirely possible he could try to take away the holdings, or perhaps worse. We need to have everything finalized as soon as possible. We are also aware of Mr. Hodges' desire to formally adopt the boy. We need to discuss that. It would be in everyone's best interests if the boy could adopt a hyphenated last name of Solomon-Hodges should he agree to the adoption. It would solidify his claim to his inheritance. It's only a formality because the DNA has been authenticated, but we want to take no chances where his father is concerned."

From the information he'd learned about Peter's father, Radon agreed about the urgency of Peter accepting his inheritance. "Let me speak with Peter and his family. I think this is a decision that requires the input of his entire family. For now, let's tentatively set a meeting at your office for nine o'clock tomorrow morning."

"That might be a problem. Since Peter's father knows where our offices are located, it might be best if we meet at a neutral location. We can talk more about that when you contact us later today."

Radon broke the connection. He, like many of his contemporaries, underestimated Drake Nivens, or whatever name he'd adopted since he disappeared seventeen years earlier.

~ * ~

Peter thoroughly enjoyed the breakfast his mother served him. Unlike the meals he'd eaten all his life, her dining table was filled with delicacies he only vaguely remembered from his early childhood.

As soon as he tasted the French toast dripping with butter and maple syrup, he was transported back to the special Sunday breakfasts his mother would prepare. During the week, there was never time for her to make anything other than toast and juice along with cereal.

"I remember eating this on special days," he declared.

Rita got a dreamy look in her eyes. "It was what we always ate before we went to church."

Peter nodded. Since his rescue, he'd been reintroduced to the One God and had been going to church. "I remember. Do you still go to church?"

"We do," Peggy answered, before her parents could say a word. "Next year I'm going to be old enough to join the church as well as the youth group. I will also be able to participate in the services."

The concept of a child of Peggy's age participating in church services was alien to him. Before he could comment, Radon entered the dining room.

"Radon," Randy greeted him. "Please join us, we have more than enough food to go around."

Peter watched his mentor to see how he would reply. He'd made it quite clear he didn't want to intrude on the family time he insisted Peter needed.

"I would be grateful. Before I could prepare my morning meal, I had a communication that I need to talk to all of you about."

Seeing Radon so serious made Peter feel uneasy.

"This sounds serious," Randy said.

Radon waited until the girls were excused and had left the room before he began speaking. He had no doubt they would be listening at the door, but it was nothing that could be helped.

"It is. I had a communication from the lawyers who represent Peter's grandfather. They are aware of your decision to adopt Peter. They would like to make things happen more quickly than going through the normal channels. The stipulation being that after Peter's adoption his last name be hyphenated to Solomon-Hodges. They feel the sooner he accepts his inheritance the better. They're afraid the publicity Peter is garnering will bring his father forward, especially once the hidden inheritance is disclosed. If he did kill his father, he did so in order to liquidate all of the family assets."

Peter felt a chill of dread go up his spine. The face of the man who took him away from his mother and proclaimed to be his father, flashed before his eyes. He could instantly feel the sting of the man's hand connecting with his face when he wouldn't stop crying. It had been his first introduction to abuse from adults. Even so, it remained imprinted upon his memory.

"Do you think he would actually come after me?" he finally managed to ask.

"Your grandfather's lawyers think so. They want to meet tomorrow morning at nine. I suggested meeting at their office, but they feel it would best if we go to a neutral location. They are afraid your father knows the location of their office and could easily find your home as well. Before I came over here, I contacted our complex here in Toronto. They feel it would be best if we were to meet the lawyers there and they have also offered you their protection until Quinton Solomon, Jr. is either found or shows himself here in Toronto."

"What about the girls' schooling?" Rita asked.

"They will be able to continue their classes, but they will have bodyguards. Of course, since Peter's break from schoolwork corresponds with that of your daughters, it will be like a vacation for them. There are many activities for them as well as for the two of you and Peter."

"It does makes sense," Randy commented. "With Peter's father being the unknown quotient, there is no need to take unnecessary risks."

"I agree, I remember how abusive he was the day he took me away with him," Peter replied. "I've seen your world. I would like you to see how I've been living since my rescue. There are wonders beyond compare."

"I've heard about the complexes," Rita said. "I never thought I would be able to experience them for myself."

"I'm pleased you are receptive to this idea," Radon informed them. "Perhaps you and the girls should get packed. I told my contemporaries at the complex about the urgency of the situation, and they agreed. Now that you are receptive to this idea, I will contact them and arrange for transportation to their location."

While Radon contacted the complex, Rita questioned Peter about the abuse he suffered at the hands of his father.

Once he repeated the story that was indelibly imprinted on his memory, he could tell how much it upset his mother. He also worried about what would happen when and if his father ever found him as an adult.

Chapter Seven

Over the past seventeen years, Seth Adamson had lost track of the number of times he'd assumed a new identity, or even the number of people who he'd made disappear because they had come too close to discovering the truth about his past. He'd been known as Seth for the past five years and was, for the first time, comfortable with his position in life. He'd added to his fortune and now was able to live comfortably on the estate he'd purchased in North Dakota. The people he interacted with saw him as a reclusive multi-millionaire.

Fortunately, he'd never trusted banks, so whenever he needed to change his identity, he was able to take his hidden fortune with him, without having to report any of it to the government or pay taxes on it. When he purchased property, it was never with the idea he would ever sell it. By changing his identity, his former homes would sit empty once he moved on.

He raised his glass of wine and thanked his father for leaving him the fortune that was the base for his accumulated wealth. With each new identity, he'd conned enough people to add to his fortune. After selling his son to Henderson Ranch, he'd perpetuated several other scams to add to the hidden money he was able to take with him. He'd tried everything from pyramid scams to selling phony stock options. Each time he was close to being outed by someone, he, along with the person who was too close to turning him in, disappeared.

Now he had enough money, he hadn't initiated any further scams. He lived a peaceful life and rarely left his estate.

The buzzing of his communicator interrupted his musings of the past. Rather than check his wrist unit, he turned on the jumbo screen. He hated trying to read or communicate on the much smaller screen.

BREAKING NEWS.

The words that scrolled across the screen piqued his interest, but he had no idea what it meant. It certainly couldn't apply to him. He'd led such a quiet life or the past five years. He was certain no one could equate him with any of his former identities.

Long-lost grandson of multi-millionaire, Quinton Solomon, Sr. has been found. He has returned to Toronto to accept the hidden fortune that was left to him by his grandfather. Peter Simes has told this reporter that he spent his life as little more than a slave, after being sold to the notorious Henderson Ranch as a toddler, and later to one of the slave ranches in Mexico.

This morning, he met with the lawyers for his grandfather to accept the inheritance that has sat garnering interest for well over twenty years, since the death of one of the richest men in Canada. He has also changed his name, and been adopted by his mother's husband, businessman, Randy Hodges.

With the Solomon holdings now in the hands of the proper heir, the lawyers predict great things for the companies included in the inheritance set aside for Quinton Solomon's first grandson.

Along with the bulletin was a picture of Peter as an adult. He would have known the boy anywhere. He carried an uncanny resemblance to his grandfather, right down to the deep cleft chin that had always been his grandfather's most striking feature.

Seth remembered his father often saying his cleft chin was why the women all loved him so much, because it was a source of unadulterated sex appeal. The fact that trait hadn't been passed on to him had always been a thorn in his side.

"Son of a bitch," Seth shouted at the now dark screen. "I was certain by selling the brat to Henderson Ranch, he would never survive to adulthood."

From what Delos told him, the punishments were harsh and the rations meager. If the brat did survive, it was entirely possible that they'd disappear into Mexico to work on one of the slave ranches he'd heard about. How dummy Delos knew all of this stuff was a mystery. The man needed someone to tell him to come in out of a rainstorm. He certainly didn't hang around with the man for his brains. It was because Seth knew Delos would do everything he was told for a little money and a lot of booze. When he fulfilled the purpose Seth had for him, there was no other recourse than to eliminate him.

Now, there was more people to eliminate than he'd ever had before. The first would give him the most pleasure, because it would be Rita. If the bitch hadn't gotten pregnant, none of this would have ever mattered.

It was only natural that he needed to dispose of his son. What a hoot that was. It was possible the bitch was sleeping with every Tom, Dick and Harry and the brat probably wasn't his son at all. With him gone, the inheritance that was rightfully his could be restored. He'd just change his appearance and go back to his birth name. He would contend he'd been unaware of this so-called son and mourned his loss. He'd also tell the authorities, as well as the media, he prayed the maniac who killed his son would be caught.

Also on his hit list were Rita's husband and any children who she might have produced, leaving no one to contest his right to the inheritance left to his son.

Next on the list were those corrupt lawyers who hadn't told him about his father's second will that hid away more of the fortune he was intitled to.

Going into super mode, he dyed his hair and beard black. To further disguise his appearance, he took out the contact lenses that would change his eye color from green to a brilliant turquoise blue. All that was left to do was to locate his intended victims.

Chapter Eight

Peter never ceased to be amazed at how fast things moved around Radon. Within an hour of his arrival at the Hodges home, they were all being whisked away to the alien complex just outside of Toronto.

The complex was almost a mirror image to the one outside of Mexico City, making Peter immediately comfortable.

In comparison, his new family seemed to be awed by the ultra-modern facility. It amazed him because he thought their home and grounds were the most luxurious things he'd ever seen. The sleek alien complex seemed stark in comparison.

It was early on the morning of the proposed meeting with the lawyers when Peter awoke. For some reason he was nervous. Even though he knew he was safe within the confines of the complex, the threat of the man who fathered him loomed in the dark recesses of his mind.

The automated system announced Radon requesting permission to enter the apartment. Immediately, Peter acknowledged the request. As soon as the door silently slid open, Radon entered the room.

"I wanted to be here with you because there is a news bulletin that will be released. I didn't want you to watch it without me by your side."

Radon's comment bewildered Peter. "What news bulletin?"

"I want you to listen to it first. Once you've heard it, I will explain all of the ramifications of it."

Peter turned on his wrist communicator and watched in horror as not only the story of his connection with Quinton Solomon, Sr. was explained but also his picture was displayed.

"Now," Radon began, "let me explain this. The authorities here in Toronto want to arrest your father. The reason we brought you here was to act as bait in an elaborate trap to capture him. We are hoping he will show up at your mother's home looking for, not only you, but the rest of your family. The RCMP officers are keeping the house under surveillance. We're hoping that in the near future, this threat will no longer be hanging over your head."

Peter didn't know how he felt about being the bait to catch his father. Unfortunately, he knew he had to go down to the dining hall with Radon for the morning meal before attending the meeting with the lawyers who represented his grandfather's interests.

~ * ~

The conference room assigned to them by the aliens who ran the complex, was small. It was evident it was meant for meetings like this where only eight people were in attendance.

Peter recognized the lawyer from the meeting at the space port, who stood at the head of the table. As the man read the conditions of the second will, Peter listened intently. It was evident these lawyers wanted him to take over the control of the companies and stocks that had been left to him. He was well aware of the fact they wouldn't be pleased when he told them of the plans he'd been making ever since he reconnected with Chris at the trial for the Grangers.

"Are you willing to relocate to Toronto permanently?" the lead lawyer asked.

Peter could feel his mouth go dry. In all his life he'd never been allowed to voice his opinion to people who he considered to be in authority.

"Who has been overseeing these assets since my grandfather's passing?"

For a moment, it seemed as though the question left the lawyers speechless. "There are managers and accountants who do that."

"Have they brought in gains in the assets?'

"Yes, they have. Why are you asking all these questions?"

"The plans I've made for my future were done before I knew of this inheritance. That said, I am not qualified for the position you have described to me. What I do know is that I love doing ranch work. The former Henderson Ranch has been purchased by the Native American side of my friend Chris' family. I have been offered the position of foreman and the opportunity to continue my education at what will be called Resurrection Ranch."

"Don't you want more out of life than physical labor?"

"Why should I? It's what I know and love. I especially want to be a part of something that will bring good to other young men who suffered while being raised by the Hendersons. We are planning to give them what they were deprived of as children, while working for an honest wage. We are hoping to help them to build self-esteem and productive lives. Not only is Chris' Native American family helping to finance this project; the white side of his family are involved, as is the family of our friend, Mark."

"You mentioned education being provided. How will this be achieved?"

"Please allow me to answer this question," Radon replied. "I think you need to know the entire story. It was Chris who first alerted the world to the atrocities being carried out at Henderson Ranch. He was a member of a white supremacy group out of Idaho who were planning to attack the complex in Denver. When he realized there were people there who wanted to help him, he defected from the group. It was then that the story of his horrific childhood came to light. He was instrumental in freeing the young men who were still being held at the slave ranches.

"During his time at the complex, he showed exceptional intelligence. It's been the same with both Mark and Peter. They were all starved for the education they were denied as children. The extent of their education was doing basic mathematics in order to make calculations for the carpentry they were taught and being able to write their names. The thought behind this type of education was that these children would be sold to one of the ranches in Mexico, so being ranch hands was more important than an education they might not ever use.

"Once Mark and Peter were located, they all started making plans for the future they wanted to build on Resurrection Ranch. Mark is going to manage the running of the ranch, while Chris will be in charge of the education for the young men and boys who will be coming for education, as well as counseling after what they've all endured while under the control of the Hendersons. They have high expectations for this venture. There are several members of the residents of the complex in Denver who have committed to relocating to Resurrection Ranch to help with the educational and medical needs of the facility."

"Those are lofty plans," one of the lawyers began. "What are your plans for your inheritance? Are you saying you are planning to liquidate your assets to finance this venture?"

"On the contrary," Peter replied.

He was thankful for the education he'd received at the Mexico City complex. With the accelerated studies and the tutoring Radon gave him over the past few days, he could speak intelligently when discussing his inheritance with these people. Together they went over the profit and loss sheets provided for each of the assets. Radon explained, in great detail, what all of the figures meant.

"From what you've told me, the assets have grown extensively. I can see no reason why things shouldn't continue as they have in the past years. As the owner of these assets, I would like to continue as a silent entity and receive a monthly or yearly check. I am not trained to be in charge of these operations, and I would much prefer working on Resurrection Ranch and doing what I love. It would also give me the opportunity to continue my education."

The lawyers looked bewildered at first, but soon their grim expressions turned to smiles. "You proclaim to be uneducated, but the way you just spoke belies that. How is it you are able to speak so eloquently?"

"Since my rescue, I have been given the best education possible. With Radon as my mentor, he has been able to explain all of the information concerning my holdings, or at least what will be my holdings when I sign the papers you are asking me to sign today."

"Well said, my boy," the oldest of the lawyers declared. "You sound like your grandfather. I was a young associate with this firm when he passed away. Still, I held him in high esteem. I'm certain no one has told you, but you resemble him more closely than you will ever know. Had your return to Canada not become worldwide news, your biological father would have no problem in recognizing you. We are grateful to the aliens for affording all of us the protection needed until he can be apprehended. Now, what are your feelings about the adoption suggested by Mr. Hodges?"

"That is something else that Radon and I have been discussing. I've also spoken to both my mother and Randy about this and, considering the inheritance and the legacy I am being offered, we agree the hyphenated name of Solomon-Hodges seems to be entirely appropriate."

Around the conference table the mood was jubilant. Peter knew his decision quelled the fears of the lawyers who worried about what the new owner of the Solomon fortune would plan to do. Peter understood the number of people who depended upon his assets for their livelihood. Years of slavery told him to never cross the people who held your future in their hands.

With the future of his Canadian holdings secure, a judge was brought in to make the adoption and name change official. For the ceremony that made Peter officially a member of their family, the two girls were brought into the conference room.

Peter smiled when he saw his sisters. *How could these strangers have become so important in such a short period of time?*

After all the legal proceedings were finished, the judge addressed the family. "Mr. and Mrs. Hodges, as of today, Peter is legally your son, as well as brother to your daughters. I pray you will always be as happy as you are on this day."

~ * ~

They had been at the complex for just under a week before there was any word about the whereabouts of Peter's father. Just after ten o'clock on their sixth night at the complex, they received news. It was confirmed that the alarm at the Hodges' home had been activated. Unfortunately, by the time the officers doing surveillance at the house could make entry, the intruder had seemingly disappeared.

Peter was encouraged when he heard there were night vision cameras in place throughout the house. It was possible he would be seeing his father for the first time in seventeen years.

Together with Radon, his mother and Randy, he watched as the footage was projected onto the large screen in his apartment.

The man on the screen held no resemblance to the man Peter equated with his father. The realization left him completely frustrated.

"It's been over twenty years since I last saw Drake, but I'd know his gait anywhere. When I knew him, he told me he had a slight limp because of breaking his ankle when he was a child."

"Are you certain?"

Rita nodded. "I don't know how I remembered that but seeing that man walk brought it back to mind. When we met, the first thing I noticed was the limp. He told me that, as a child, he'd been horseback riding and fell trying to make a jump. Even though he had the best care available, he was a defiant teenager and didn't do as he was told, and it didn't heal correctly."

"I remember that accident," one of the lawyers said. "Quinton and I were in the same class in school. Everyone knew who he was, but as far as he was concerned, we were nothing more than dirt under his feet. His father was rich, and he never let anyone forget it. The accident happened during the summer break and he was training to be in a horse jumping competition.

"Being teenagers, we were delighted to think how far the mighty had fallen. He didn't take the teasing well and vowed he would ride in that competition one way or another. In other words, he didn't do what the doctors told him, therefore hindering the healing of his ankle. The next disappointment he had was when his father forbade him to compete. That could have been the catalyst for his motive to murder the old man. From everything I've heard, he blamed his father for him not being able to compete even though it was the injury and not his father that kept him from doing so. Because of his foolishness, he was not only unable to compete, but he did more damage, causing the ankle to not heal properly."

"You knew my father as a teenager?" Peter asked.

"Knew of him, but I didn't really know him. My father worked for the city department of sanitation. In other words, he picked up garbage. Being ultra-wealthy, your father thought I was too insignificant for him to associate with me."

Peter could feel a new rage growing toward his father. Although he only knew the man for a matter of hours, even at the age of three, he had seen evil radiating from him.

~ * ~

Seth entered the home of his former girlfriend and knew immediately there was no one there. Was it all a ruse for him to show himself? Were they all in hiding somewhere? This certainly wasn't going according to his plan. He'd planned to be in and out within a few minutes to plant the explosives that would go off and destroy, not only the house, but also the lives of at least five of the people he needed to get out of his life.

Instead of carrying out his plan to plant the explosives, he left the house. No one would ever know he'd been there. One way or another he would find, not only Rita, but also his son. Now, more than ever, they both had to die.

Under the cover of darkness, he made his way back to the wooded area where he'd left his hovercraft. As he lifted off, he could see several official hovercrafts landing around the house, which was now bathed in the light of their spotlights.

"Damn," he said aloud. "They must have had a silent security system."

Lifting off, his mind went wild. *I got out of there just in time. I'll need to be more careful in the future. The next step will be finding out where they're hiding.*

~ * ~

Peter was still reeling from the pictures he'd seen from the night vision cameras when the officers came into the apartment with more footage. This was from the trail cams that were located throughout the wooded area of the property.

Once it was played on the screen, the footage showed a hovercraft landing and the man who entered the house stepped out. It seemed like an eternity before the man returned. Thankfully, it was long enough for several cameras to observe the craft and show the registration number painted on the side panel.

It was a great relief to have this footage. It would help in identifying the craft if it were spotted anywhere within the province. Quinton Solomon, Drake Nivens, or whatever name he was now using, would soon be apprehended and the dread that filled them ever since Peter learned the true identity of the paternal side of his family, would be gone from his life forever.

"This is only the beginning," Radon cautioned. "We know who we're looking for. We also have the identifying marks on his craft, but he could be holing up anywhere. I have a feeling he's not dumb enough to check into a local hotel. He must know we are looking for him, considering the amount of police presence that was at the house."

~ * ~

Seth reconsidered his options. He was pleased to think he'd had the presence of mind to find a remote area in the forests of the Upper Peninsula of Michigan to make a rude campsite. If they were looking for him in the Toronto area, they would be out of luck, because he would be out of their reach in a different country.

All he needed was to lay low for a couple of days until all of this blew over. He would take the time to rethink his strategy. Maybe it would be for the best if he returned to Toronto as Quinton Solomon and say he'd heard about his long-lost son who had now been found.

The more he thought about it, the crazier the plan sounded. He was wanted for kidnapping, or at the very least, interfering with parental custodial agreements. He didn't know if there was a statute of limitations in cases like these, but he wasn't willing to take the chance.

I'll think about this tomorrow, he vowed. *It's been a long day and I need to get some rest.*

~ * ~

The longer they went with no sightings of his father in the area, the more apprehensive Peter became. What if they were never able to leave the protective custody of the complex? For the first time, he wished he'd never been found. By returning to his mother's life, he'd put her entire family in danger of being found by the man who he now knew murdered at least two people in addition to kidnapping Peter when he was but a small child.

Depression was threatening to take over, when Radon, Randy, and Peter's mother requested to be admitted to his apartment.

"We have news," Randy announced.

Peter looked up, apprehensively. "News?"

"There are reports of a man matching the description of the intruder into your parents' home camping out in the woods of the Upper Peninsula in the state of Michigan," Radon explained. "The state police have been alerted and are planning to surround his campsite in the morning. Since the first murder that we know of took place here in Toronto, he will be extradited back here to stand trial. We are hoping they can also incorporate the charges of kidnapping and the murder of Delos Reynolds. It wouldn't matter where he is tried. The punishment if he is convicted is the same. Life imprisonment on one of the penial colonies either on the dark side of the moon or under the ice cap of Antarctica. Either way it's a death penalty."

Peter remembered when the sentence of life imprisonment under the ice cap of Antarctica was handed down to Pops and Ma. If was as if hearing the sentence was the most horrible thing either of them expected.

"If there is a trial, I want to be there," Peter declared.

"As well you should," Rita agreed. "I know I want to be there. Because of that man, I suffered for many years wondering what had become of the little boy who disappeared without a trace from my home."

Peter ached for his mother. Although he had longed to be with her, he never thought of her hurting as well. From the moment he arrived at Henderson Ranch he'd been told his mother was a dirty whore. Even so, he'd missed her loving touch and the meals she made for him.

Chapter Nine

Seth turned over in his sleeping bag. He missed the luxury of his bed in his North Dakota estate. Overnight, he'd made the decision to return to his home. Wherever his son and that bitch Rita were, it was possible he might never find them. Let the brat have the old man's fortune. From what he'd heard about the kids that went to Henderson Ranch, he wasn't competent enough to handle the amount of money he would be inheriting.

It was entirely possible the money, as well as all the holdings, would be squandered within the first year. That was where he and the brat were different. He'd taken all the money he could out of the accounts and hidden it well. Not only had it allowed him to live well over the years, but some of his investments had made him a tidy profit. He had money squirreled away throughout the United States under the names he'd acquired and used over the years.

He was just preparing to fix his breakfast when the woods came alive with the sound of people coming toward his campsite.

"Quinton Solomon, put your hands in the air. We have a warrant for your arrest."

"Th-there's some mistake here. You have the wrong person. My name is Seth Adamson. I'm here on vacation from North Dakota. As a matter of fact, I was planning to return home today."

"We have your image on footage from a home invasion in Canada. We also have a report of your hovercraft being in the same area at the same time. Once we get back to the station, we will have a doctor come in and read your DNA chip. That will be the definitive decider of just who you actually are. Now, you are to come with us."

Seth tried to think fast. The last thing he needed was to have someone read his DNA chip. Just being called Quinton Solomon sent a chill of dread up his spine.

"I tell you—you have the wrong person. Let me get my identification. It's in the tent and…"

"And nothing. You are coming with us and all of your belongings will be confiscated and brought to the station."

"What about my hovercraft? You can't just leave it here?"

"We have enough officers with us. One of them will be able to bring it back to the station. We have already contacted the authorities in Canada as well as those in Montana and Missouri. It seems like you've been a busy little boy. Let's see, there are charges of murder in Toronto, kidnapping in Missouri and murder in Montana. I have no doubt of your guilt."

"I have absolutely no idea what you're talking about," Seth lied.

He was thankful they didn't know about the other murders he'd committed over the past twenty years. He was also thankful the death penalty had been abolished with the coming of the aliens to Earth. All he had to do was to con the courts into believing he was completely innocent on all the charges they were alleging he was responsible for.

With the electronic cuffs around his wrists, he had no choice but to allow the officers to push him toward the waiting hovercrafts in the clearing just beyond his campsite. Rather than dwell on the here and now, he allowed his mind to wander to the murders he'd committed over the years.

The first, of course, had been his father. Who knew that old bastard would have withheld a major portion to be left to the brat who should have died years ago? It had been so easy to kill him. He'd played the grieving son to the hilt and refused to have an autopsy done. It was the only way anyone would have known that his father didn't die of natural causes.

With that experience, it was so much easier to do away with Delos. He was so dumb that he never expected his 'good' friend wanted him to disappear forever.

Next came the woman in Illinois who wouldn't go to bed with him. As much as he pursued her, she wouldn't give into his charms and pressure. It didn't hurt that she had no family and no one to miss her. He often wondered if anyone ever found her body in the cave where he'd hidden it along the Mississippi River.

Over the next years there were other women who wouldn't have sex with him, as well as businessmen who came too close to the truth about who and what he was.

North Dakota had been a new start for him. With his reclusive lifestyle, he allowed no one to get close to him. Whatever he wanted or needed, he was able to order and have delivered either by delivery people or drones.

A sudden feeling of dread went through him. With his hovercraft in custody, he knew it would take only a minimum of time before they were able to trace him back to his North Dakota estate. What they would find if they searched his home might incriminate him further.

Why in the hell did I think I needed to get rid of that bitch Rita and her brat? If I'd stayed put, none of this would be happening.

He knew the answer. It had been too long since the last time he'd had the thrill of murdering someone. The thought of ending so many lives at the same time gave him a high. It was in his blood. It was what he needed.

~ * ~

After last night, Peter hadn't slept. He wondered if the authorities had apprehended his father. How would he feel when he saw him face to face? Seeing him on tape was one thing. It was quite another to see him in the flesh.

He remembered how it felt when he first saw Pops and Ma. Over the years they'd dominated his nightmares, along with his father and Delos Reynolds. They all represented his demons and eventually turned into the monster's children worried about finding under their beds.

The clock read a little after seven thirty when the automated system announced Radon was at the door, requesting entry to the apartment.

"It's over," Radon announced as soon as the door closed behind him. "The Michigan State Police surrounded your father's campsite and arrested him just after dawn this morning. He's being transferred to Toronto as we speak."

The stress of the sleepless night, combined with the relief of knowing his father posed no threat to him or his new-found family, overcame him. Unable to speak, he felt himself losing consciousness.

He had no idea how long he'd been out, but when he came to, his apartment was crowded with concerned people. A doctor checked his vitals and his mother clung to Randy, crying softly.

His first instinct was to get up, but the doctor insisted he lay back and rest. "What do you think prompted this?" the doctor asked.

"It has to be the stress of what's been going on for the past few days. I didn't sleep last night."

"The news I brought this morning made him relax for the first time in several days," Radon added.

Peter nodded. Knowing his father was in custody and no longer a threat brought about a peace he hadn't felt since the day his father took him away from his mother's loving home.

"We've been in contact with the authorities," Randy said, "and they tell us we won't be able to confront your father until tomorrow at the earliest."

"That's good, because I want this young man to rest," the doctor advised. "I'm certain arrangements can be made for his meals to be delivered to the apartment."

Peter wanted to protest, but Radon was already ordering the morning meal for all of them to be delivered. From the corner of his eye, he saw his mother leave the room, and presumed she was going to bring the girls in to be with them. It was best they were all together for the remainder of the day. It would be good to get better acquainted without the worry of what would happen when and if the monster of his dreams found them.

Their breakfast was delivered almost as soon as his mother returned with Peggy and Jenny.

"This is so exciting," Peggy declared. "It's like we're having a picnic. Eating at your apartment is going to be so much better than going down to the dining hall."

Peggy's childish excitement was not lost on Peter. He could feel something he'd missed by growing up on Henderson Ranch. For the remainder of the day, he enjoyed the carefree feeling of being a child and getting to know his sisters. How he wished he'd been able to have them in his life from the day of their births.

Chapter Ten

Seth sat in the cell he'd been assigned. In his youth, he'd watched many old movies that were made in the twentieth century. In them, jail cells had iron bars. It wasn't the same with where he was being kept.

It looked as though he was in a wide-open room, but he knew there was a force field keeping him confined. He read enough about law enforcement to know of all the technology being used in the big cities. Until now, he wasn't certain there would be such modern advancements in effect in the rural jails.

Since his arrival, the day before, he'd seen no one other than the guards who came to bring him meals. They always came in force. One man brought the food while two others stood guard. Both of them were heavily armed with laser guns. Any wrong move and his life would be over. He knew he needed to stay calm if he wanted to beat the charges that were being levied against him.

"Do you really think I'm such a dangerous man?" he asked.

He knew the officers heard him, but none of them made any comment. It was certainly because every move he'd made since being incarcerated had been caught on the camera mounted high above his head in the corner of the room. It was degrading to know they were filming him taking a leak. He hoped they were getting a thrill out of watching him remove his penis from his pants.

"When you finish your breakfast, your lawyer is here," one of the guards informed him.

"What lawyer? Who did you call? I didn't ask for any damn lawyer. Why should I? This is all a sham. When are you going to realize you have the wrong person? I've told you over and over again that my name is Seth Adamson, and I was merely on a camping trip. Had the officers arrived any later, I would have been halfway home."

"Tell it to your lawyer. It is what you are entitled to, although if it were up to me, I'd push you into the force field and end it all. It would save the province a lot of money."

"Now officer, you know they have you on tape. You could lose your job."

"Not if I only voiced my opinions. I'd suggest you eat up and don't keep your lawyer waiting too long."

~ * ~

The local sheriff, Alistair Coburn, approached the secluded estate of Seth Adamson. From all accounts, the man was a very wealthy recluse.

The opulence of the exterior of the home came as a surprise. Most people lived a more sedate life in rural North Dakota.

It didn't take long to open the door. As soon as he entered the house, an alarm started going off. Ignoring the annoying beeps of the alarm system, he looked until he found the panel for the controls of the system. It didn't take much to disarm it. The whole thing made him wonder if an alert was being sounded at his station.

Once everything was again silent, he directed his deputies to begin searching room by room. He concentrated on the great room that dominated the entire first floor.

Off to one corner, a massive desk took up the majority of the back wall of the room. None of the drawers were locked so he was able to go through each of them methodically. What he found was nothing short of a treasure trove.

In the top center drawer, he found pilot's licenses with at least ten different names, each issued from a different state or province with the same picture and description of the owner. The man was a master at being able to change his identity. Along with the pilot's licenses were other papers to confirm his identification. It was possible, he'd forged all of these papers.

After putting everything into an evidence bag, he explored one of the other drawers. In it, he found a computer backup drive. Thinking it might be worth having his technicians look into, he added it to the evidence bag.

The next drawer netted him a gun with ammunition, and still another drawer held several large knives.

This guy was ready to hold off a siege if someone came to get him. What I want to know is who the hell he actually is?

By the time they finished searching the house, his officers had confiscated enough weapons to arm a small army. They'd also brought four computers, three communicators, and numerous bags of papers to the great room.

Before leaving the property, he placed a call to Federal Police to meet him at the station. Once he was assured that they were on their way, he also called the Mounties who were investigating things in Canada. This case was far larger than his small force was prepared to deal with. With his limited personnel, it would take him weeks, if not months, to go through everything they'd confiscated while at the property.

~ * ~

Being such a small community, word spread like wildfire that the police were out at the Adamson estate. As soon as the convoy of police vehicles pulled onto the main street, Alistair saw what looked like the entire population of the town lining the streets, as though in anticipation of their arrival. While he flew in his hovercraft, several of his officers drove the antiquated solar powered trucks in order to bring back all the confiscated items from the estate.

I feel like this is a damn circus parade. Are they expecting me to start throwing candy out to the kids? Who would have leaked the information to everyone in the damn town? He didn't need an answer to his question. The amount of police vehicles that had headed out to the estate early this morning had to be an indication that something big was going down. *It's not like there hasn't been a lot of speculation about Seth Adamson ever since he first built the estate everyone thought was far from the norm for the area.*

Docked at the station were hovercrafts from the federal and state authorities. He was grateful for the extra help he would be receiving in unloading all of the items they'd pulled out of the Adamson estate.

"I'm Captain Lukas Ferguson, from the Federal Office in Bismarck. I'm anxious to see what you found out at the Adamson estate.

"You should be," Alistair replied. "I know my men found a cache of weapons, along with several computers and communicators. If you brought any IT experts, they could get started on them while we're cataloging the weapons. Of course, what I found in the desk is also quite interesting. I found identification and pilot's lenses from several different states and provinces with the corresponding paperwork to substantiate the man's identities. I have a feeling this goes deeper than any of us ever thought it would."

"I tend to agree with you. Considering he killed not one, but two people in the past, why should he do anything different, especially with all the identifications?"

"It's a shame we'll never know what he's been doing for the past seventeen years since he left Montana."

The look on Lukas' face told him the man expected to glean enough information from what they'd brought in to piece together the activities of on Seth Adamson, or whatever his real name was.

Two hours later, one of the IT techs came into Alistair's office with a broad smile on his face.

"Do you have good news for us?" Lukas asked.

"I think the two of you will want to see what we found. This guy was writing a novel and I doubt if it's fiction. He describes, in great detail, two murders, and there are at least a hundred pages we haven't read. The first murder was committed while he was under the name of Quinton Solomon, Jr. and the second under the name of Drake Nivens."

Alistair and Lukas both nodded their heads. "Those are the two murders that are being investigated in Canada and Montana. It will be interesting to read the rest of the manuscript. I have a feeling it will clear up several cold cases around the country."

Alistair completely agreed with his contemporary from the federal level. "Once we have read the remainder of the manuscript, it's highly possible there will be no need for a trial. From what I've read about other trials, the Council of Intergalactic Affairs takes a dim view of any hint of murder. We both know they are the ones who supervise the penal colonies on both the dark side of the moon and under the ice cap of Antarctica."

Lukas sat quietly for a few moments. "I've never been a fan of the Council of Intergalactic Affairs, but in this case, I'm more than happy to turn over the punishment of this perp to them. If it were up to me, I'd kill the son of a bitch with my bare hands. It was bad enough when he was being investigated for two murders and kidnapping his own son. I have a feeling what we're about to uncover will be a whole other kettle of fish and believe me, it will smell just as bad."

Chapter Eleven

Peter felt rested when he awoke the next morning. A day with family and most of it spent resting was exactly what he needed. He knew this morning would be a trying experience, to say the very least.

He'd been glad of the plans for Radon to spend the night on the pull-out sofa in the living area of the apartment. As much as he wanted to be alone, he knew the fact his mentor was only a few feet away at all times came as a reassuring concept.

Even though his father had been in custody in Toronto for two days, he'd been advised not to see the man until this morning, giving him time to meet with his attorney. He knew it was the law that his father be given counsel, but if it was up to him, he'd convict the man without a trial. If he were stronger, he even considered killing the man with his bare hands.

"Did you sleep well?" Radon asked when Peter entered the living area.

"Better than I have in years."

"Good. We're to meet your family in the dining area. Once we've all eaten, we will be going to the detention center to see your father."

The mention of seeing his father sent a chill of dread down his spine. *I want to face him and yet I don't want to see him. How do you face the monster of your dreams?*

Without putting voice to his concerns, Peter simply nodded. He'd been waiting for this moment for too many years to back out now.

~ * ~

Rita, Randy and the girls were waiting for them when they entered the dining hall. After filling their plates from the bountiful buffet, they seated themselves at a round table for six at the far side of the room.

Although everyone at the complex knew the reason they were staying there, no one made mention that there had been any connection with the lead story that had been on the news ever since his father's capture.

"Can we go with you today?" Peggy asked.

"I'd rather you didn't," Peter replied, before his mother could say anything. "I don't even want to go, but I have to. It's no place for respectable young ladies like you to be. I'm certain Radon has made arrangements with some of the people here to keep you occupied while we're gone."

"But..." Peggy protested.

"But nothing," Rita said. "You heard your brother. This is going to be hard on him and he wants to spare you. I totally agree. If I could spare him, I would, but he knows he needs to do this to bring closure."

Peter thought the girls would argue further, but his mother ended the discussion. From what he remembered, his mother's words were always law. There were no punishments but there didn't have to be. He respected her too much to ever go against her will.

They were just finishing eating when a young woman came to their table. She squatted down between the chairs where the two girls were sitting.

"My name is Sira. I'm the director of the children's activities here at the complex. Today, the children who live here full time are going to the botanical gardens for a field trip. With each season the theme for the gardens is changed. Since it's spring, there are many beautiful flowers. Do you girls think that is something you might be interested in doing?"

Peter watched as the girl's eyes lit up with excitement. This was evidently something different from their usual routine. He wished he could go with them and promised himself he would make a trip there before it was time for him to go back to Mexico.

~ * ~

Still maintaining his name was Seth Adamson, he paced the cell. Earlier, the guards who brought him his breakfast told him he would have more visitors today. After meeting with that fool lawyer yesterday, he had no desire to see anyone else.

The digital clock read ten in the morning when the guards reappeared. He knew they would deactivate the forcefield to take him to the meeting room. The thought crossed his mind to try and escape, but he knew he didn't have a snowball's chance in hell. Even if he got past the two guards, there were always two more with laser guns ready to cut him down if he tried to escape.

"Who do I get to see this time?" he asked. "I hope that fool lawyer isn't coming back again. The only thing that son of a bitch could say was to throw myself on the mercy of the court. Why in the hell would I do something like that? I'm innocent, and I've been telling you that ever since you brought me here."

"Keep telling yourself that."

The guard who delighted in tormenting him roughly placed the electronic cuffs on his wrists. Without waiting for him to adjust to the tight cuffs, they escorted him down the hall to the room where he'd met with the lawyer the day before.

As soon as the door opened, he came face to face with the people who were responsible for him being in this mess. Rita was as beautiful as she had been the first night he had sex with her. How was it possible that over twenty-one years had passed, and she hadn't aged?

The man beside her had to be her new husband. From the look in his eyes, Seth was positive if there hadn't been protective barrier, the bastard would have come across the table and assaulted him.

Rather than concentrating on Rita and her new husband, he turned his attention to Peter. There was no denying they were father and son. If he didn't have the facial hair or the contact lenses, his green eyes would have been a dead giveaway. As for the cleft on the boy's chin, it matched the one in his father's chin perfectly. Even the boy's red hair was identical to his before he had dyed it days earlier.

Beside the boy was a man who could only be one of the aliens who seemed to be everywhere. He stood well over six feet tall and had piercing lavender eyes along with silver hair.

"So, you're Peter Simes," he said. "It's a shame they have the wrong person. I'm not your father."

"The name is Peter Solomon-Hodges. Like hell you aren't my father. I would have recognized your voice anywhere. I should, I've heard it in my dreams ever since you took me away and had your friend take me to Henderson Ranch. My question for you is why?"

Why? The brat wants to know why. How could he understand what the thirty thousand dollars Henderson paid for him meant to me? Most of my money was tied up in investments. I needed it to start my new life in Illinois.

"Aren't you going to answer me?" Peter shouted. "Maybe you can't hear me through the glass. Do I need to shout louder?"

"I didn't answer you because I had no idea what your father's motive might have been. Whatever it was it has nothing to do with me. Like I keep telling people, my name is Seth Adamson. None of the idiots here will listen to me."

"Why should they?" the alien said, speaking for the first time. "Before this meeting, we met with the doctor who read your DNA chip. It is a perfect match to Quinton Solomon, Jr. It also proves you are Peter's biological father. In other words, you are guilty of kidnapping your son and selling him to Henderson Ranch. Now are you going to give your son the answer he wants?"

"If I were his father, which I doubt, it probably would have been for the money. From what I've read, that old man paid good money for boys he could get to do his work for him."

"How much money?" Peter pressed.

"From what I heard, thirty thousand dollars."

The look on his son's face was sorrow, mixed with anger and disbelief. For a moment, he was sorry for what he did to his son, but the money had been worth it.

"I can't take any more of this," Peter declared. "If I thought being with Henderson and then on the slave ranch was unbearable, they can't hold a candle to sitting across from this piece of shit. I'll see you at the trial if you even get one. With what you're charged with, the Council of Intergalactic Affairs might not hold a trial before they take you to one of the penal colonies. If that's the case, I hope you are treated like I've been all my life. In other words, may you rot in hell."

Peter got to his feet and turned his back to the partition. From his outburst, it was evident he had a temper to match his red hair. He'd always blamed his temper on his red hair. At least the kid got something from him.

~ * ~

Peter left the conference room. Seeing his father close up had brought back every nightmare he'd experienced over the years. Even with the black dye in his hair and beard, Peter could see the red hair growing out at the base of his beard.

"Damn," he shouted, punching the wall. "Why do they have to have a trial? The man is guilty as sin."

"It's the law," Radon assured him. "Everyone is entitled to a fair trial. It will be hard, but you'll get through this one, like you did the one in Nevada. Once this is behind you, your life can begin. Keep thinking about the role you'll be playing at Resurrection Ranch along with your friends, Mark and Chris."

The mention of the ranch and doing something he was good at, calmed the temper that had started building within him. At this moment, he wanted nothing more than to be riding a horse on the open range. Doing the work for a good cause would be much more rewarding than it had ever been before.

"You're right, of course. Being angry doesn't solve anything, but when I think about what that man did to me, not to mention the two murders he committed, I can't help it."

"I can understand," Rita said, coming to his side. "I don't want to be patient and wait for the legal system to do their work. There's no way he can deny anything now that his DNA has been confirmed. He's in denial. From what I see, he's been conning people for so long, he wouldn't admit the truth if it slapped him in his face."

~ * ~

After seeing his son and Rita, he couldn't deny his identity much longer. The thought of life imprisonment at one of the penal colonies was almost more than he could fathom. It would be for the best if he could end his life, but with the guards watching him day and night, along with the ever-present cameras, committing suicide was completely out of the question.

He knew he was only trying to deceive himself. He could easily commit suicide by trying to step through the force field. He had to admit he was too much of a coward to do something like that. He didn't want to feel the pain that would accompany such an attempt.

Chapter Twelve

Before Peter, Rita, Randy and Radon could leave the building that housed the jail where his father was being kept, one of the guards stopped them.

"The commander would like to speak with you before you leave. You can follow me to the office."

As they prepared to follow the guard, they exchanged questioning glances. "What do you think the commander wants to see us about?" Peter whispered to Radon.

"It's obviously something to do with your father. I'm certain we will find out what it is soon enough."

Peter agreed and followed the guard as they made their way through the maze of corridors to the office of the commander who requested their presence.

To everyone's surprise, rather than an older male officer, the commander was a woman of about thirty years of age.

"Welcome," she said, getting up to greet each of them personally. "I'm Amanda Barrett, the commander of this facility. We have just received information on prisoner 364356. In other words, Quinton Solomon, Jr., or whatever alias he prefers to go by. I thought it was something the four of you would be interested in hearing."

"Anything about the man is of interest to myself, as well as my friends," Radon replied.

"I'm pleased to hear you say that. Make yourselves comfortable as this will take a while."

Peter and the others seated themselves in the room, which resembled a stately home, rather than the office of the commander of an impressive prison facility for criminals awaiting trial.

"Yesterday, the law enforcement from the town closest to the estate of our prisoner, in North Dakota, entered the estate and did a complete search. What they found was eye opening. To begin with there were enough various weapons to equip a small army. At least that is the way the authorities there put it. They also found identification under several different names. In following up on these leads, they discovered unsolved murders in each area where the identifications were issued. The most damning information of all, was the novel he was writing. It was saved on several stick drives as well as on computers. When they first called us, they'd only read far enough to confirm the murders of Quinton Solomon, Sr. and Delos Reynolds. They are certain they will learn the identities of at least ten other victims. Considering all of these murders took place in several states and provinces, the case has been turned over to the Council of Intergalactic Affairs. It will save the cost of individual trials in the states as well as Canada. All of the charges will be consolidated into one case.

"I thought it was imperative for you to know this. If you want another meeting with him, it should be arranged soon, since he will be transferred to the Denver complex for his trial."

"I have no desire to ever see him again," Peter said. He knew his tone was filled with venom. "Although, I understand I will have to testify against him at his trial. From what I've heard, my mother and I might be the only people who could identify him. I am also probably the only eyewitness to at least one of the crimes he committed. I will never forget the man who kidnapped me from my mother's home and sold me to the monsters at Henderson Ranch. I'd just as soon send him straight to hell, but Denver will have to do."

"I agree with my son," Rita said. "With the exception of the two of us, he's been able to cover his tracks completely. He's clearly good at removing any witnesses. I'm certain he thought Peter might not survive childhood and I would never be able to find him. Thank the One God that Radon was able to match Peter's DNA to mine and bring about our reunion. It's also good to know the publicity surrounding it gave Drake, as I knew him, the opportunity to tip his hand in trying to get rid of both of us. Had none of that happened, he would still be living as Seth Adamson in North Dakota and nobody would have been any the wiser. He tripped himself up and deserves whatever punishment he is given."

Commander Barrett nodded her head in agreement. "I can understand your feelings. He has wronged both of you gravely. If I were in your position, I would harbor the same feelings. I would have been remiss in my duties, though, had I not apprised you of these new findings and given you the opportunity to see him again before he is taken to Denver. I'm told the transfer will be taking place at the beginning of next week."

"We thank you for your consideration, Commander, but today has been draining for both my wife and my newly adopted son. With the trial that will undoubtedly be held soon, I feel it is best if they do not have a repeat of this morning's confrontation."

~ * ~

To say Seth was shaken by the morning's meeting with Rita and Peter would be a gross understatement.

The boy, although he still showed symptoms of the starvation and ill treatment he'd experienced throughout his life, was no doubt his son. Of all of the people on Earth, they were the only two who could identify him. True, there were probably men who were his childhood friends who might remember him, but it was hard telling where they were. Without Rita and Peter, he would have been home free.

He damned himself for being selfish enough to want the two of them out of the way. If he'd let sleeping dogs lie, he wouldn't be in this predicament.

"Are you ready to admit to your real identity?"

He looked up to see an attractive woman standing just beyond the force field that separated him from his desired freedom. If circumstances were different, he would have tried to seduce her and take her to his bed. Of course, that wasn't possible, with the cameras watching him twenty-four-seven. He always prided himself on keeping his affairs secret from the world. It made killing his conquests so much easier.

"I don't know what you're talking about," he replied, his tone as sarcastic as possible. "I keep telling everyone that my name is Seth Adamson. Just who are you to question my word? Why don't any of you believe me?"

"I can answer your question. To begin with, my name is Amanda Barrett. I'm the commander of this facility. I received word from the authorities in North Dakota saying they have raided your estate. They have found all of your false identification, along with the cache of weapons, and the manuscript you are working on. There is no doubt you are Quinton Solomon, Jr., Drake Nevins, Seth Adamson and several more names that I haven't been given so far. There will be officers from the Council of Intergalactic Affairs coming at the beginning of next week and you will be transferred to Denver for a consolidated trial. From what I've been told, all of the principalities involved have agreed to this. It would be for the best if you were to admit to your crimes and avoid the trial altogether."

Seth weighed his options. They had him dead to rights, but there was still a chance he could fake his way through a trial and convince the judge and jury of his innocence.

"Do what you want. I keep telling you I'm Seth Adamson. How my chip got confused with Quinton Solomon, whoever he is, I have no idea. Someone screwed up and it wasn't me."

~ * ~

"Are you prepared to go to Denver?" Radon asked, once they were on their way back to the Toronto complex.

"I am," Peter replied. "You must know, my friends, Chris and Mark are both there. I'm certain you can arrange to be with me so I can continue my education."

"That I can. What about you, Rita?"

"I can be there for the trial, but no longer. I have responsibilities here. You know, my job, the girls, my husband. I can't pick up and leave for any extended period of time."

"That's understandable. It's possible this will be a long, drawn-out trial. No one would expect you to be there for the entire process. The same goes for you, Peter. You could return to Mexico as soon as you testify, but I have a feeling you want to see this through to the end. The fact your friends, as well as mine, are at the Denver complex makes our relocating there an easy process. It's different for your parents."

Peter didn't miss the look of pride on Randy's face when Radon referred to them as his parents. He knew he was finally proud to have been found by his true family. He certainly didn't consider the man they'd seen in the conference room his father. He was nothing more than a sperm donor.

"Now that we know what's going on," Randy began, "I would like to tell you what I've been working on. I didn't want to say anything when we thought Peter might stay in Canada, but since we know he has his heart set on returning to the ranch in Nevada, I feel the time is right. For several months now, I've been thinking about opening a branch office in the States. As far as I'm concerned, there's no reason why I can't find a location close to the ranch where Peter will be working. The office here in Canada has a good staff and I'm thinking of promoting James Fenton to office manager. He does most of the manager's job now and I have great faith in him."

Rita thanked her husband over and over again for being so concerned with her happiness to open a new office close to where Resurrection Ranch would become Peter's home. For Peter it was a dream come true. The thought of leaving his mother so soon after he found her was overwhelming. Having her close enough to visit any time he wanted to, was something he never envisioned happening within his lifetime.

"I never asked, what kind of a business do you have?" Peter was finally able to ask.

"I do online accounting for various small businesses here in Canada. I've had several requests from companies in the States. To be truthful, I've been researching this for several months. Since everything is done online, I have no qualms about where I open an office. If things go as well in the States as they have in Canada, it will be a successful move."

"I think you've made a good decision," Radon commented. "I

have several good contacts in the States, many of whom are contemplating moving to Resurrection Ranch. One of them is Cassion. He has one of the finest legal minds in the galaxy. He can be of help in setting up your business. He is also going to be part of the legal team for the ranch. It's amazing how many people are offering their help to get this project going. It's entirely possible the ranch could be your first client in your new location."

Randy beamed. "I was hoping that we could become part of this new venture. For better or for worse, it looks like you're stuck with us, Peter."

"I wouldn't want to be stuck with anyone else. It looks like each of us are bringing good backing to this project."

"What do you mean?" Rita asked.

"It started with Chris. The Native American side of his family purchased the ranch, while the white side has pledged financial backing. Mark's family is also backing the project financially as well as offering to open a school for veterinary medicine on the ranch. Now I have something I can offer as well. With the money from my paternal grandfather, I can help with the financing. Your offer to do the accounting for the ranch is an added bonus."

~ * ~

It seemed as though plans materialized almost out of nowhere. Peter was amazed when his sisters were as excited about the move as his parents.

"Aren't you sorry to be leaving your friends here in Toronto?" Peter asked.

"We can always stay in touch." Peggy assured him. "Now that we have a big brother, we don't want to be so far away from him."

Peggy's statement warmed his heart. Even though he knew when he left for Denver, he would be leaving his newfound family behind, he understood when the trial was over and he returned to Resurrection Ranch, he would never be separated from his family again.

Chapter Thirteen

Peter was torn as their craft took off for the flight from Toronto to Denver. On one hand he was anxious to see his friends but on the other, he didn't want to be separated from the family he'd only so recently found.

The amount of security at the Denver complex was mind boggling. Even Radon was surprised by the number of armed personnel who seemed to be around every corner of the docking area, as well as the complex itself.

"What's going on?" Radon asked when Cassion met them.

"We had an urgent request from Commander Bennett in Toronto. She wants Solomon out of her custody as soon as possible. They have thwarted at least two suicide attempts in the past twenty-four hours. I informed her that you would be arriving early this afternoon, so our troops arranged to make the transfer just after your flight left. They should be arriving within the next two hours. By that time, you and Peter should be secure in your accommodations. I know Chris and Mark are anxious to spend time with Peter."

"Where will my father be held?" Peter asked. "Will it be secure, or should I be afraid of him escaping and finishing what he wanted to do in Toronto?"

"Those are good questions," Cassion agreed. "Although he will be landing here at the complex, as soon as he finishes the intake process, he will be relocated to a secure location outside the complex. In the past, that location was a maximum-security prison. I've done some research on it and learned that the most dangerous prisoners were housed in an underground bunker. Just recently, it was refurbished with all the modern security amenities. The prison bars have been installed with security cameras as well as a force field that is many times more secure than that they have in Toronto."

Peter breathed a sigh of relief. In no way did he want to be in the same building or even the same complex as his so-called father.

~ * ~

When Peter arrived at the apartment he'd been assigned to, he was surprised to find Chris and Mark waiting for him. Having seen Chris only a few weeks earlier, he had no trouble recognizing him. As for Mark, he was but an older version of Marco, the little boy who joined them at Henderson Ranch when they were little more than toddlers. Over the years, they'd worked and played together, sharing their hopes and dreams for the future. Back then, none of them ever envisioned what the future held for them. Peter knew he and Mark dreamed of working for top wages in Mexico. How different everything turned out.

Chris was always the one who had no concrete plans for his future. Although he worked the ranch, Peter knew it wasn't something he enjoyed as much as his friends did. As Peter recalled, Chris was a confused young man, with no idea what his future held.

While they were in Nevada, Chris told him of his desire to work with kids and young adults. The plans for Resurrection Ranch seemed like the ideal solution for all of them. With Chris overseeing the education and counseling of the boys who would be coming to the ranch, and Mark as manager, he would be very comfortable as the foreman.

To be reunited now, before the stress of the trial, gave Peter a chance to relax and renew the friendship the three of them enjoyed throughout their childhood.

"You're looking good, Peter," Chris said, as soon as he entered the apartment. "You know that Mark and I have both changed our names. Have you decided to shorten yours?"

"I honestly haven't given it much thought. There's been too much going on."

"I can understand that." Mark commented. "We've been

following everything about your biological father on our communicators. That's a lot to digest, in and of itself."

"There certainly has. Meeting my mother after all of these years was emotional enough, but when her husband wanted to adopt me, it was completely overwhelming. Now instead of being Peter Simes, I'm now Peter Solomon-Hodges. I belong to a real family and have two younger sisters who are delightful. They are all planning to move from Canada to a location closer to Resurrection Ranch. They will be close to me for the rest of my life."

"It seems like there's a lot of that going on," Mark said. "When I attended the trial for my father and grandfather, I found I had a half brother and sister. They are planning to relocate to Resurrection Ranch with their mother and my paternal grandmother. I have a feeling Resurrection Ranch will be a complete family project. For now, let's go down to the dining hall and celebrate. I'm ready to enjoy the evening meal and to be truthful, the food here is exceptional."

Peter laughed at Mark's comment. As kids, it was always Mark who liked to talk about the food he enjoyed eating and couldn't partake in at the ranch. From what Peter could tell, Mark was no longer talking about food but eating more than he actually needed. It was good to see his friend was enjoying his life, now that he'd been rescued.

Before they could begin to talk about the plans for Resurrection Ranch, the automated voice of the emergency alert came over the intercom connected to every room in the complex to tell of any emergency in the area.

Alert, alert. Please shelter in place for the next hour as a dangerous prisoner will be docking and taken to the secure facility adjacent to the complex. There is no immediate danger, this is a precautionary order only. When the all-clear is issued, you will be alerted.

"Is that your father they're talking about?" Mark asked.

"I'm afraid so. When I arrived, there was an overabundance of security guards. They told me it was because my biological father would be arriving. I saw him once when he was being held in Toronto and that was enough to last me a lifetime. Even though he is a very charismatic man, I can't stand to be in the same room with him. I dread the trial that is coming. As far as I'm concerned, he's far worse than the Hendersons or Pops and Ma. This man has intentionally killed at least twelve people. I know there were a lot of kids who died at Henderson Ranch, but for some reason, that's different. This man not only killed and hid his victims, but also changed his name, and moved to another location to carry out his heinous acts within another area."

"I guess you're right. Kids are expendable, at least that's what the Hendersons thought," Chris commented. "None of us had anyone who would miss us, or so we were told. I can't believe the love I've received since I found both the white and the Native American families."

"I agree," Mark said. "Finding my mother's family as well as my paternal grandmother, my stepmother and my siblings, has been very interesting."

The expression on Chris' face was one of sadness. "I envy the two of you being able to find siblings. Since neither of my parents survived the crash of their hovercraft, I found family, but it's not the same. I would have loved to have found either a brother or a sister."

Peter understood. Even though he only recently found his family, he remembered when he thought he'd been forgotten by his mother. In the past he'd imagined his mother moving on with her life and being happy without him. How wrong he'd been. She'd kept his memory alive in her heart and passed it on to her new family.

"Let's not dwell on this current emergency," Peter recommended. "Hopefully, there will be no problem with the transfer of the prisoner to the secure location. I'm anxious to see what you have planned for Resurrection Ranch."

Chris got up from the chair where he'd been sitting and went to the desk on the other side of the room. He laid out the plans on the table, as Mark and Peter joined him.

"This is the photographic image that came across my communicator of the current condition of the ranch."

Peter took the picture from Chris. He was appalled by the difference only a couple of years had made on the ranch where he'd grown up. He wondered how it could have deteriorated so much since he left.

"The elders of the reservation where my mother grew up have already started the demolition of many of the outbuildings. There will be a new dormitory built along with individual houses and a high-rise apartment complex. The main house, of course, is still in excellent condition. We agreed that Mark's stepmother, as well as his siblings, will be moving into it, since they will need more space than the rest of us. From what I've heard, Mark's paternal grandmother will also be moving into the main house."

"How many people are you planning to bring to the Ranch?"

Mark answered his question. "From this complex, Dr. Gratan, Kara, Cassion, Hodia, Chris, Melian, and Lego, along with Caroline, Aaron and their baby. Of course, my grandmother as well as my stepmother and siblings are also coming."

"What about other kids that grew up there? Unfortunately, most of the kids who were sold to Señor Alfanso didn't live more than a couple of years. I only know of a handful of others who made it. How any of us survived is a mystery. Was it the same with the ones who were sold to the ranch where you were, Mark?"

"I'm afraid so. We do have a listing of the names of some of the kids who are either at other facilities or unaccounted for. We were hoping, as the foreman, you might be able to track them down and convince them to return to the ranch for education and rehabilitation."

Peter contemplated the suggestion Mark made. He'd never considered his role to be more than the foreman of Resurrection Ranch. Chris' role as head of the education and rehabilitation program and Mark's position as ranch manager, were well defined. Until only moments earlier, he thought his role was set in stone, but now he saw that not only would he be the foreman, but it would entail working daily with the young men who would be joining them.

"It makes sense. I would like to know the hands on a personal basis before they arrive at the ranch. Never, in my wildest dreams did I ever think I would be able to help find these young men and boys. It will give me a leg up to know them before we begin working together. It's entirely possible not all of them would be interested in the ranching end of the business. As I recall, Chris, you were never happy working with the cattle."

His comment brought laughter from both of his friends.

All clear. I repeat all clear. You may return to your normal activities.

Peter could feel the stress drain from his body. The 'all clear' order meant his biological father was in the secure facility and no longer a threat to anyone at the complex.

"So, where do we start looking for these kids?" he finally asked.

"Cassion gave me a list of names that were found when the ranch was raided. Some of them are the younger kids who were rescued and are being educated at the Nevada complex. They're the ones whose families couldn't be located. Thankfully, there are only three of them who haven't been claimed by the families they were stolen from. One of the things we learned was that the majority of the kids who came after we did were kidnapped and sold to the Hendersons in the same way as you were. As for the others, they could be anywhere, from working with groups like Patrick Ernst's or on the ranches in Mexico. Do you think this is something you can handle?"

Peter looked at the list Chris handed him. The three kids that were in Nevada were Dan Campion, Brad King, and Norman Priestley.

He immediately recognized Clint Anders, Parker Flint, and Roger Blount. They were older than him and had all been sold to Señor Alfanso. Since they had been liberated at the same time as he was, he knew he could find them at the Mexico City complex. It wouldn't take much to convince them to join him at Resurrection Ranch.

Those who were unknown were Ken Raspier, Dennis Salinger, and Jerry Wallace. It would take some digging to find their whereabouts, but he was certain he was up to the challenge. His newfound wealth gave him access to one of the finest legal teams in Canada. If anyone could find these men, he was certain the investigative personnel of his legal team would be able to do it. Once he was settled, perhaps as soon as tomorrow, he would contact the head of the firm and give them the three names of the missing men. They would be able to begin the process of locating them.

With the logistics of finding the future residents of Resurrection

Ranch in place, Chris pulled out the plans for the new buildings to be erected, including the apartment complex, the dormitory, the dining hall and the outbuildings.

"We have been assured the cattle and horses left behind by the Hendersons are of the best bloodlines. It's no wonder they showed a good profit for all those years. Cassion was able to look at their books and they were bringing in over five million dollars a year from the sale of not only the stock, but also kids like you and Mark. They also profited from the support money provided by the state of Nevada."

"That's mind-boggling," Peter said. "Just from the cattle, we will be able to make a good profit. At the same time, we will be helping these other kids to begin their new lives."

~ * ~

After meeting with his friends, Peter was more than ready for a good night's sleep. He knew his work would begin first thing in the morning and he wanted to be well rested before starting.

Radon met him at the dining hall and was as excited as Peter had been about the plans for Resurrection Ranch. "It sounds like you'll be jumping into this project with more responsibility than you thought earlier. How do you plan to find the three young men that haven't been located?"

"The lawyers from the law firm in Canada have told me they would be willing to help me in any way possible. I contacted them before I came down for breakfast and they already have their investigative team looking into it. Hopefully, they can be located before we're ready to begin operations."

"You've grown up a lot since we first met on that ranch in Mexico. I think you're going to do well. You probably won't be needing me at all."

"Like hell I won't. As my mentor, I'm afraid you're stuck with me. I wouldn't be nearly as prepared for this next stage in my life without your guidance. I still need a lot of education and I am certain you will be a great asset when the other men arrive at the ranch."

"That's exactly what I wanted to hear, I look forward to being a part of this project, especially since my friends Cassion and Hodia are already invested in it."

"Changing the subject," Peter continued, "I know my father arrived here yesterday. Have you heard anything about when the trial will be held?"

"Cassion and I held a meeting about that last night. As soon as all the murders were uncovered, his team began preparing. They've been in contact with the authorities in the areas where the murders took place and arrangements have been made for them to be here with their witnesses a week from this coming Monday. He anticipates the trial lasting for at least one, if not two weeks. It is entirely possible there will be little deliberation by the jury, since he has completely outlined each murder in the book he was writing. I have a feeling that will be the most damning witness against him."

Peter breathed a sigh of relief. The sooner the trial was over, and his father was sentenced to the punishment he deserved for the crimes he committed over the past twenty-five years, the better.

"Do you think my family can be here on such short notice?"

"I contacted Randy and Rita as soon as I finished talking with Cassion. They were already planning to get ready to leave Canada and begin looking for a place to relocate closer to Resurrection Ranch. They were pleased that they would be able to spend some time with you before leaving for Nevada. Everything is working out perfectly."

Peter thought about the other trial that weighed heavily on his mind. "When will the trial for Señor Alfanso and Hank be held?"

"That's something else I was meaning to talk to you about. I had a communication from my counterparts in Mexico last night. They said Señor Alfanso suffered a heart attack. He was found unconscious in his cell three days ago. Even though he had the best medical care, they weren't able to save his life. He died within hours of being found. As for Hank, when he heard about Alfanso's death, he pleaded guilty and asked for mercy. After he confessed all of the things he was made to do to the slaves, he was sentenced to life in one of the facilities in one of the most remote areas of Mexico. There is no chance he will ever be paroled. You will not have to face either of them again."

Peter felt tears begin to pour from his eyes. It wasn't that he grieved for either Señor Alfanso or Hank. They each got the punishment they deserved. Instead, his tears were ones of relief. He was thankful that he would not have to ever face the tormentors who had made his life a living hell for the past two years.

Chapter Fourteen

Peter sat in the courtroom, surrounded by his family, as well as Radon, Chris, Mark, and the legal team from Canada. Even with so much support, he could feel his stomach begin to roil at the thought of seeing his father enter and take his seat at the defendant's table.

Unlike when they met in Canada, the black dye had grown out, showing the red roots that looked so much like Peter's own hair color. With the man's beard shaved, the resemblance between the two of them was remarkable. The only difference he could see was his father didn't have the deep cleft in his chin. Otherwise, the man was almost an exact replica of not only Peter, but also his grandfather. It made Peter sick to his stomach to think he looked so much like this man who had perpetuated so many heinous acts.

The first witnesses called by the prosecution were the lawyers from the Toronto law firm.

"Do you recognize the defendant in this case?" Cassion asked.

"Yes, although I knew him as a young man. This is definitely Quinton Solomon, Jr. I was but a junior associate in the firm, but I knew his father as well as the son. When I rose in the ranks within the firm, I took over the affairs of Mr. Solomon, Sr., including the secret will leaving half of his assets to any grandson who may, in the future, come forward to claim it."

"What can you tell us about the passing of Mr. Solomon, Sr.?"

"Everything was rushed and Mr. Solomon, Jr. had his father buried before he even contacted the firm regarding his inheritance. He'd even brokered selling the house and furnishings before he came to our office demanding what was left to him in the will. Prudently, we never mentioned the second will for assets for his son."

"When an heir was found, what did your firm do?"

"We went to the authorities and had Mr. Solomon Sr's body exhumed. The autopsy, which should have been done at the time of his death, was performed. At the time, the son wouldn't give permission, and with good reason. It showed that the father had been suffocated, making the death murder rather than of natural causes."

"I have no more questions for this witness," Cassion concluded.

The defense attorney stood to begin his questioning of the lawyer. "Do you know who the murderer was?"

"Not for certain, but by his actions, the man sitting at the defense table is the only one who had reason to want the old man dead. As his only child and surviving heir, he assured himself he would be receiving all of the family assets. That, added to the rush to bury his father and leave Canada, allows for little or no question regarding his guilt."

Rita was the next witness to take the stand. "How do you know the defendant, Mrs. Hodges?"

"I knew him as Drake Nevins. I thought we were in love and allowed him to have sex with me. He is the father of my son, Peter."

"Was he a good father?"

"As soon as I told him I was pregnant and the child would be a boy, he disappeared. I didn't hear from him again until Peter was three years old. That was when he came to my house and kidnapped him."

"How do you know it was my client?" the defense attorney questioned.

Rita held up the paper she'd brought to the stand with her. "The daycare workers told me Peter's father came to pick him up. When I got home this note was waiting for me. It reads 'You've kept my son from me long enough. He's with me now instead of his mother who is a whore. Don't look for us because you won't find us. Drake.' I kept it in the hopes that one day I would find my son. At the time, the authorities couldn't do anything because Drake was Peter's biological father. Until recently I'd given up all hope of finding my son, but I never destroyed this note. Now I know why I kept it."

Even with only two witnesses, it was time for the judge to call for a recess for the noon meal.

Peter could tell his mother's testimony had been draining for her. Rather than taking her to the communal dining room, Peter insisted luncheon be ordered and brought to his apartment. Radon agreed. He arranged for the meal to be delivered and sought out the girls so they could join with the rest of the family.

"Are we having a picnic?" Jenny asked.

"I guess we could call it that," Peter replied. "With the high profile of this trial, I decided I didn't want to be the center of attention. Mom is drained and I need time to prepare for my testimony this afternoon. Besides, I wanted to see the two of you more than anyone else in this complex. Radon agreed with me. I have a feeling you'll find that Radon is more of a family member than a mentor."

Radon beamed at the compliment. Just by watching the man, Peter could tell his mentor cared deeply for the family he'd found only weeks ago.

~ * ~

Peter was the first witness of the afternoon session. As he got to his feet to take the stand, he could feel his stomach threaten to rebel. He was beginning to wish he'd skipped the noon meal.

"Would you please state your name and how you know the dependent?" Cassion asked.

"My name was Peter Simes and is now Peter Solomon-Hodges, and the defendant is my biological father."

"What is the meaning of your last name?"

"My father disappeared from my mother's life before I was born, therefore I was given her name at birth. When we were reunited, her husband was generous enough to adopt me and give me his last name. At the time of the adoption, the lawyers for my grandfather's estate insisted I incorporate his last name."

"How do you know my client is your biological father?" the defense attorney asked.

"When I was three years old, my father picked me up at the

daycare center. He told me he was going to take me on an adventure. Instead, he turned me over to his friend, Delos Reynolds, who took me to Henderson Ranch. I was old enough to understand when money changed hands. What I didn't know was that I wouldn't be allowed to be given a proper education, to say nothing of being used as practically slave labor. When I turned eighteen, I was sold to a ranch in Mexico. If I thought where I grew up was a hell hole, it couldn't hold a candle to working for the man who bought me. For anyone who thinks slave labor is a thing of the past, they are sadly mistaken. I thank the One God for sending the representatives from the Alien complex outside of Mexico City to rescue me, along with the other slaves on the Alfanso Ranch."

"How can you be certain this man is your father?"

"I knew the minute I heard his voice. It's the same voice I've heard in my nightmares throughout my life. That coupled with the match of our DNA, there was no question. Today, seeing him clean shaven with his hair growing out and showing its red roots, there is no denying the fact we are father and son. Believe me, if I could erase this man from my life and my DNA, I would. He has been the monster of my dreams for far too many years."

Following Peter's testimony, people who knew his other victims took the stand and told of how they knew Quinton Solomon, only under a different name. They told how friends and loved ones disappeared only days before he could no longer be found in the area.

Peter wanted to vomit when the people testifying told of the brutality of the murders in their communities as well as how the bodies were purposely hidden from view. It was evident the capture of his father had cleared up many old cases from several different states and provinces.

The testimony took almost a week before the defense put on their case. It came as no surprise that the defense had no character witnesses.

Peter watched as his father took the stand. The man who looked out across the gallery and prepared to give his testimony, was charismatic con man who duped so many people for far too many years.

"Would you state your name, please?" the defense attorney asked.

"My name is Seth Adamson and I have an estate just outside of Fargo, North Dakota."

"What about the other names we've heard you called throughout this trial?"

"They have me confused with someone else."

Peter wanted to jump up and object to what his biological father was saying. It was Radon who stopped him.

"Give him enough rope and he'll hang himself," Radon said.

The archaic quote meant absolutely nothing to Peter. "What?"

"It's an old saying I came across several weeks ago when I was researching crime and punishment in the early United States. It was said that in that time and place, murderers and horse thieves were punished by hanging by their necks until dead. It was said the executioners used a stout rope to carry out the ultimate punishment. In other words, his own testimony will be as damning as anything we've heard so far. Let the law run its course."

Peter turned his attention to the jury. With every lie that came from his biological father's mouth, he could see the members of the jury becoming as disenchanted with the testimony as he was.

At long last, both sides gave their closing arguments. As Radon predicted, the jury only deliberated for two hours before reaching their decision. When the word guilty was read out, Peter could see the weight of the world descend upon his father. The sentence was handed down just as quickly.

Two guards, wearing the uniform for those serving as personnel at the penal colony on the dark side of the moon, came into the room to take the convicted man away. Never again would Quinton Solomon, Jr. breathe the air of Earth or enjoy the sunshine. For the rest of his life, he would be nothing more than a number and a prisoner at the penal colony.

Although Peter thought he was going to be relieved once the sentence was read, part of him worried about the stigma that would follow him for the remainder of his life, through the DNA coursing through his veins, linking him to Quinton Solomon/Drake Nevins forever.

Chapter Fifteen

Peter stayed at the Denver complex for a week following the trial. He was thrilled to be given the chance to take care of his sisters while his parents flew to Nevada to look into places to relocate close to Resurrection Ranch.

Together with Radon, they'd explored the entire complex and met many of the people who would be living and working on the Ranch when the time was right for them to relocate.

Mark told them about his younger brother and sister and was certain they would become fast friends. It made the girls all the more excited about moving to the United States and being closer to Peter.

By the end of the week, it was evident everything was working out for the best. Peter spent two days with his parents and saw them off at the docking station when they prepared to leave for Canada to close up their lives there and begin their new adventure.

~ * ~

After saying goodbye to his family, Peter prepared to return to Mexico City. He was anxious to meet with Clint, Parker and Roger. If things went as he planned, they would be willing to join the others from Henderson Ranch at Resurrection Ranch.

After docking, Peter and Radon went to their former accommodations to shower and change into clothing that weren't travel stained, before going to meet the three friends who had been sold to the Alfanso Ranch, just as Peter had.

It was apparent Radon had already contacted each of them, as they were waiting in the dining hall.

"Peter, it's good to see you, man," Clint greeted him.

Although Peter knew Clint, like himself, was fluent in Spanish, he was relieved his friend chose to speak in English. It was the language he'd been speaking ever since he landed in Canada several weeks earlier.

"Where have you been?" Roger asked.

Peter proceeded to tell his friends about meeting his parents and helping to convict his biological father for unspeakable crimes against not just him, but the twelve people he was guilty of murdering.

"Why come back here?" Parker inquired. "Why not stay with your family?"

Peter explained about the project at Resurrection Ranch and how he wanted them to be included in the project, not only to make the ranch prosper but to continue their educations.

"You say Christopher and Marco are behind this?" Clint pressed.

"They're the ones who started it, but I am behind it one hundred percent. The Native American side of Chris' family actually owns the ranch, and his white family is backing it financially. Mark's paternal grandmother along with his stepmother and siblings are relocating there to help with the educational needs, while his maternal family is adding financial backing as well as starting a school of veterinary medicine. That brings us to me. My paternal grandfather left me a very wealthy man and my mother's husband, my now adopted father, is moving his accounting business closer to the ranch. We're going to be one of his first clients."

From the expressions on the faces of his friends, he knew he'd overwhelmed them with the information. He wondered how they would feel when they learned of the number of aliens who were willing to become part of the project. Their educational and medical backgrounds would be more than beneficial to all of them.

"What would we be doing?" Roger finally inquired.

"Whatever you enjoy doing. We will need ranch hands, people to help with the younger children, as well as those of you who are perhaps interested in entering the medical field. There are many opportunities open to anyone who is willing to work for them. Along with the work, there will be a great opportunity to complete your education. I know you've all been getting an education here and we plan to continue it at the ranch."

Parker gave him a quizzical look. "What it is you enjoy doing, Peter?"

"I've been offered the position of foreman. It's something I know I would be good at. I could have chucked the whole thing and moved to Canada to run the companies my grandfather left me, but I have no desire to sit behind a desk. I know you're all good ranch hands, but if there is something else that you're interested in, no one would fault you for following a different path."

"I don't feel as though I have enough education to know what I want to do with my life," Parker admitted. "If I sign on as a ranch hand, will I be allowed to change my mind when and if I decide to do something else? Another thing, what about food? Will it be the same swill we were given when we were kids?"

"I can assure you, there will be three nourishing meals a day. There will also be dedicated school hours. If you're anything like me, you are already taking accelerated courses. Chris is the one who is involved with the educational side of things. By the time we get to the ranch, he'll be married to Melian. She's one of the aliens and from what he's told me, an excellent teacher."

"How many aliens will be there?" Parker asked.

"Let's see, Cassion is a lawyer, Hodia works with the youth, Dr. Gratan is going to run the medical facility along with Kara and Logo, who are both nurses. We'll be hiring personnel from the area to help with everything. I have a feeling Mark and Kara will be married, if not before they arrive at the ranch, then shortly thereafter. Of course, my mentor, Radon will be coming with us."

"Are you looking to marry one of the aliens?" Roger teased.

"To be truthful, I haven't landed in one spot long enough to meet anyone I would like to spend my life with. Chris met Melian when he first went to the Denver complex. It was evident they were attracted to each other from the beginning. As for Kara and Mark, she was his nurse when he was rescued. You know the shape we were all in. From what I'm told, he was close to death when they brought him to Denver. If it hadn't been for Dr. Gratan and Kara, Mark might not be with us today. I'm not sure if he knows he loves her, but I could see the attraction between the two of them."

Peter knew they were getting away from the topic of Resurrection Ranch, but at least the conversation had lightened up somewhat.

"You don't have to give me your decision today. I know it's hard to think about returning to that hell hole where we grew up. I knew it was for me. It was Chris who told me things were going to be entirely different when we get there. I saw pictures of the place, and the dormitory as well as many of the outbuildings have already been bulldozed down. The new construction is due to start within a matter of weeks. To begin with, you would be bunking in the dormitory, the same as me. Chris and Mark will be having apartments in the high-rise apartment building that's being erected."

"It sounds good to me," Parker said. "You can count me in as a ranch hand, until I figure out what I want to do with my life."

Roger nodded his head in agreement.

Peter knew if Parker agreed to come to the Ranch, Roger would follow suit. They'd been close when they were children and had both been sold to Alfanso at the same time. The truth be told, Parker was the intelligent one of the two of them, the leader. Roger was always willing to follow no matter where Parker led him. The wild card in the group was Clint. Even though he fit in with everyone no matter what group he was with, he was happier going in his own direction.

"You can count me in, too," Clint said. "Everyone here has been good to me, but I need more than being confined to the complex. I miss working with the cattle, even though I don't know if that's what I want to do for the rest of my life. How soon can we leave?"

"Chris is getting married soon. Once the festivities are over, Mark will be leaving for the ranch. Chris will arrive within the next two weeks. I'm certain we can make the arrangements for the three of you to come sometime after that. I still have three of the younger boys to talk to as well as three that no one has been able to locate. My lawyers in Canada, as well as Hodia from the Denver Complex, are working to find them. Once they do, I'll be talking to them as well."

"Who are you still looking for?" Parker asked.

"Ken Raspier, Dennis Salinger and Jerry Wallace. Do you remember them?"

"I'm surprised you don't remember them. They were at the ranch when we were. They were older, of course. I heard Henderson grumbling about them not being fit to take to the ranches. He said there was a group he called the skinheads. As I recall, he said the same thing about Chris. I don't know if that's any help, but it's all I know."

"How did you happen to hear that?"

"I've always been one who listened to everything Henderson said, especially when I was a kid. I liked knowing things no one else did. If Henderson knew I was listening to what he said, he would have beat the shit out of me."

Peter remembered the stories Chris told him about the treatment he'd had from the militant group he joined in Idaho. He hoped he could get through to these other young men and persuade them to come to Resurrection Ranch. He wanted them to be part of the process to rebuild the ranch.

~ * ~

With the knowledge that his friends at the Mexico City complex were willing to come to help with the rebuilding process, Peter was encouraged as he made his way to the Nevada complex where the younger children were being housed.

As children, he wondered how they adjusted to the fact that the majority of their peers from Henderson Ranch found families who had been looking for them for many years, when they had not?

Each of the children had been orphans whom the state decided were better off at the boys' ranch than in an institution. How wrong that assumption had been. During their time there, they'd been starved, given severe punishments and seen their friends die because of mistreatment. Peter was glad none of them had been called upon to testify against the Hendersons. From what he heard, it was hard enough for the adult survivors. He was also thankful he hadn't been found in time for the trial of the Hendersons. The trial for Pops and Ma was difficult, even though he didn't have to testify. Had it not been for Radon, it might have broken him. Instead, he'd grown as an individual, by meeting Chris and learning about Resurrection Ranch.

The people in charge of the Nevada complex were very warm and welcoming. Like all of the other complexes he'd visited, his apartment was more like a luxurious hotel room.

The morning after his arrival, he and Radon were escorted to the area where the classes were being held.

The first child to be brought into the conference room was Norman Priestly. Peter didn't remember him, but he rarely remembered the younger children and this boy would have been barely six when Peter aged out.

"Hi, Norman. How are you doing?"

"Good."

"How do you feel about being here at the complex?"

"I'd rather have a family or…"

"If Henderson Ranch was changed, would you be willing to come there to live?"

Fear was the only word Peter could think of to describe the look in Norman's eyes.

"Are the Hendersons still there?"

"No, they aren't. The ranch has been sold and is under new management. Once you are there you will be treated well, get enough to eat, and be able to work on your education."

"Will I be able to ride horses?"

"You will, after your schoolwork is done. A lot of the people who will be running the ranch are former residents. I was there from the time I was three and I will be the foreman. The manager lived there from the time he was four until he aged out. Last but not least, the man you'll be working with was sent there when he was just a baby. None of us thought we had any family, but a wonderful woman by the name of Hodia managed to find family for all of us. She will also be working with you."

"Do I have to leave my friends, Brad and Dan?"

"Absolutely not. I'm going to be talking to them next. We want to bring as many men and boys back to the ranch as possible to better prepare them for the future. I know you each have a mentor here, just like Radon is my mentor. I want you to talk to them and see what they think about what I'm proposing. We want to give you a future. As for the education, all of us are continuing our studies while we're working on the ranch. We were all deprived of the tools to be productive adults as kids. You're lucky. You're young enough that the learning will come much easier for you than for us. It's a great opportunity."

It was hard to read Norman's reaction to what he'd said. From what he'd been told, all three of the boys he'd be talking to today were ten and eleven years old. He didn't remember them, but like Clint, he'd much preferred his own company, even though he enjoyed the company of Chris and Mark. As for the younger children, like the kids older than him, they were just there. He'd never bothered to get to know any of them on a personal basis.

The next child he met was Dan Campion. This boy was far different from Norman. Rather than having anger brewing just below the surface, Dan seemed to be an easy-going child.

"Would I have to work on the ranch? I like riding the horses, but the cows scare me."

Peter nodded. This kid sounded more like Chris than himself. "What do you like to do?"

"I've been talking to my mentor and I told him I'd like to learn to cook. He said I might be able to become a chef, like the ones who cook the meals here."

Peter smiled. "I have a feeling the cooks in the kitchen at the ranch would be more than willing to teach you everything you want to know. If you decide there's something else you want to do, you will have the opportunity to train for that as well. Like I told Norman, I want you to talk this over with your mentor. I know he's meeting with my mentor, so if there are any questions, he can answer them."

The last child to be brought into the conference room was Brad King. Peter immediately knew he was the leader of the three. He was neither easy-going nor angry. He was a natural leader and Peter knew he would have to capitalize on that.

"So, you're Brad," he greeted the child as he entered the room.

"I remember you. You're Peter. I thought you were the greatest when you were still at the ranch."

Peter was caught off guard. "Why do you say that?"

"Because you were so good at what you did. Why are you here?"

Peter went on to explain about Resurrection Ranch and the project that would be starting in a few weeks.

"Do you want me to come there?"

"We'd like all three of you come, but only if you want to. We're prepared to offer you an education as well as a good work ethic. How do you feel about ranching, like we all did when we lived there?"

"I can take it or leave it. I don't know exactly what I want to do, but I know I don't want to be a ranch hand all my life. Would I have a choice to do something else if I wanted to?"

"You bet. Not everyone is cut out for that life. I talked to Dan and he wants to learn to cook, and I assured him he would be able to work in the kitchen."

"Dan? Cooking? Where did that idea come from? Are you trying to tell him what he wants to do?"

Brad's questions caught Peter off guard, but he tried not to show his shock. "Believe me, I would never try to tell anyone where their lives should go. I recently had someone who wanted me to stay in Canada and administer the companies my grandfather left me. At the time, I know it would have made them happy if I would have agreed. I know my mind and I completely understand I don't have the education or the ability to take on such responsibilities. My love is ranching and as the foreman of Resurrection Ranch, I can do what I enjoy and continue my education. Maybe, someday in the future, I might decide I want to do something else, but for now, I'm content working as the foreman."

"When do you need for us to give you an answer? I want to talk to the others as well as our mentors. I mean, we have it pretty good here. We don't have to do any work other than our studies. I don't know if I want to go back to ranching. That was damn hard work."

Even though the expletive was mild compared to other words he'd heard throughout his life, it came as a surprise to hear the child say such a thing. From his experience at the complex in Mexico City, he knew the aliens didn't approve of such language. For now, he wouldn't make a big deal out of it.

"It is hard work. I can understand if it's not something you would enjoy doing. There will be several other chores that will need doing. I'm certain if ranching isn't to your liking, the counselors will be able to guide you in the right direction. As for when I need an answer, I don't want this to be a snap decision for you. I'll be here for the next week or so, as I am waiting to hear back about some other young men who might or might not be in this area. Either you or your mentor can find me."

He quickly wrote down the information concerning his apartment number and location. He watched as Brad picked up the paper and looked it over. Hurriedly, the boy shoved it into his pocket. The action caused Peter to wonder how his education was coming along at the complex. It was evident Brad had no idea how to read what had been written.

He knew without the education and leadership Radon gave him, he would have had a hard time reading anything that was written. It was entirely possible Brad's cocky attitude was a cover-up for a learning disability. He made a mental note to contact Chris when he returned to his apartment and see what he thought.

"I'll talk to our mentor and let you know."

Peter held out his hand to Brad, but the boy turned defiantly away from him. It was evident he'd taken on the role of leadership for his friends in order to mask a disability he was unwilling to admit to having.

As soon as Peter was certain the boy had gone back to his quarters, he decided to go in search of the teachers at the facility. If his assumptions were correct, they would certainly be able to tell him how they were handling his educational needs.

~ * ~

It was late when Peter finally arrived back at his apartment. Meeting with the teachers had shed light on the problems that seemed to be following Brad even after leaving Henderson Ranch.

From what he learned, there was a disability that prevented him from learning like his counterparts. The teachers said they had carried out some tests and had reached the conclusion that the severe punishment doled out by the Hendersons had arrested his mental growth. They were working on a program to meet his needs and reverse the effects of the life he'd been living before being rescued.

Even with the late hour, Peter opened the screen on his communicator and placed a call to Chris.

"It's good to hear from you. How are things going in Nevada?"

"I talked to all three of the younger kids who are here without any family. Two of the boys were very accepting of the offer, but the one who seems to be the leader, Brad King, might prove to be a problem. I talked to his teachers and they assure me he isn't as far along in the educational process as the others. They have decided it was because of some of the punishments he received when he was younger. Do you remember him? He said he was six when we aged out of the program."

From the picture on his communicator, he could tell Chris was trying to remember the youngster they were talking about.

"I think I do. He was probably three or four when he first came to the ranch. As I recall, he was a born leader, but he was also an angry kid. He stood up for the other kids who were his age and often took their punishments on himself. Do the teachers have a program we should be following when and if he relocates to the ranch?"

"They do. I gave them your name as well as Hodia's. They're working hard to come up with a plan to reverse the effects of the punishments he was given."

"I hope so. If Melian and I weren't in the middle of the plans for our wedding, I'd like to come down there and meet with him. Keep me posted on how things are going. In the meantime, I'll give Hodia a head's up about Brad. I do appreciate you doing this for us."

"Not a problem. Has anyone been able to locate the last of the three missing men?"

"Hodia is working on that too. She thinks she has a line on the group they're affiliated with. Hopefully, we'll be able to meet with them since they're somewhere close to our location here, I'm leaving that up to

Mark and Cassion. I'm sure they would appreciate it if you could be here, but it sounds like you have your hands full with the younger kids."

"If I can wrap things up here soon, Radon and I will come up to your location. I do want to be there for your wedding."

They talked for several more minutes before breaking the connection. Once they did, Peter realized just how tired he was. Luckily, he'd eaten his evening meal earlier, so he was more than ready to go to bed.

Once he fell asleep, his mind produced nightmares of the life he'd led on Henderson Ranch. Within an hour of retiring for the night, he was awake, drenched in sweat. He needed to talk to someone, but at this late hour, who would it be?

As if Radon knew what was going on with him, the automated voice announced that his mentor was at the door, requesting entry to the apartment.

Without hesitation, he gave the command for the door to open. Although he had no idea how his mentor sensed his need for the two of them to talk, he was pleased to have the opportunity to speak with Radon and try to ease his mind about the youngsters he'd spoken with hours earlier.

"I sensed your restlessness. Would you like to talk about it?"

Peter nodded. "I had a nightmare about my life on Henderson Ranch. When I spoke with those young boys, I realized they lived through the same hell as I did. I am afraid history might repeat itself. What if we aren't able to give them the education they deserve, while still running the ranch? What if we become as abusive as the Hendersons were?"

Radon nodded sagely. "I can understand your concerns. What you have to realize is that you are not in this alone. With Chris, Mark and you involved, you understand the pitfalls. Each of you has shown remarkable intelligence and have mastered the classes you've been attending with unprecedented speed and accuracy. Since each of you have mentors, there is no way the past will be repeated. I have a feeling one of your main concerns is Brad."

"You're right. Brad is a concern. After speaking with his teachers, it's evident the injuries he sustained at the hands of the Hendersons could be an impediment when it comes to not only his education but also his future. I worry about his inability to grasp the lessons he's being taught."

"I worry about that as well. I spoke with Hodia earlier this evening and she would like to have Brad transferred to Denver as soon as possible. They have a research team there who have been working with children with learning disabilities. She would like to have him evaluated by her staff and given a plan for his future. It's entirely possible this problem could be resolved through their program."

Peter contemplated what Radon said. "Do you think he would agree to the transfer?"

"In the morning, I will contact the mentor for all three of the boys. We can meet with them and suggest the transfer for all of them at the same time. It seems as though Brad is the leader of these kids. I can't imagine tearing the three of them apart. We can explain that even though the educational opportunities at this complex are exceptional, there is a wonderful counseling program in Denver they can participate in. If they all think the counseling will help them to readjust to their new life away from Henderson Ranch, it will make their transfer easier to understand."

"That just might work. The rest of us have been away from there for several months, if not years. For these kids, it's only been a matter of weeks. I realize the hurt and the pain is still fresh in their minds. I know it comes back to me every so often in my dreams."

Radon smiled. "Like tonight?"

Peter nodded. "There are many nights when the nightmares are so vivid, I have to force myself back awake to be assured I'm away from there as well as from Señor Alfanso. If it's so close to the surface for me, how much worse must it be for them? I'm older and I understand what has to be done to have a future. The minds of these kids are still growing."

"You have grown up since we first met. I don't think you have to worry about repeating the past. For now, it's time for you to sleep. Tomorrow, or I should say today, is going to be a long and trying day. If everything goes as planned, we could be transferring to Denver with the boys either this afternoon or tomorrow morning."

With everything that was running through Peter's mind, he wondered if he would be able to go back to sleep. Lovingly, Radon reached out and touched a spot at the base of Peter's neck. As soon as he did, Peter found he could no longer hold his eyes open. Sleep without dreams or nightmares came instantly.

Chapter Sixteen

Morning sunlight flooded Peter's bedroom when he awoke. A glance at the clock told him he'd slept until after ten in the morning. The last thing he remembered was talking to Radon about Brad and his friends. At the time, they had been sitting on the couch in the living room. Now as he awoke, he realized he was in his bed. Had their conversation been nothing more than a dream?

Getting up, he made his way to the bathroom to begin his morning routine. After relieving himself, he washed up and shaved.

Once he was dressed, he walked into the living room. To his surprise, Radon waited for him.

"Did you sleep well?"

"You know I did. What exactly happened last night, or should I say early this morning?"

"We had a good talk about the boys who are being considered for their return to Resurrection Ranch. We came up with a plan and I knew you would need your rest before we put anything into action. I used a trick I've learned over the years to ease your mind so you could get the rest you needed. Had you not awakened on your own, I would have roused you within the hour. We have a meeting set up between us, the boys and their mentors for noon."

"Have you had any sleep?" Peter inquired.

Radon laughed at the question. "You tend to forget, my needs and yours are entirely different from one another. Being from the dark side of the moon, our days are when we sleep and nights sometimes last forty-eight to seventy-two hours."

Peter had given no thought to such a difference. "How will this affect my father? Being human, what will the effects of such a change mean for him?"

"The area of the colony where the people from Earth are imprisoned have artificial light to turn night into day. We have found that to have to adjust to our day versus night pattern would be far too difficult for them. They are sent there for punishment, not for inhumane treatment. It is enough that they are expected to do hard labor for the rest of their lives. That is enough for you to know for now. We need to get to the meeting with the three boys and their mentors."

Peter tried to envision his father doing hard labor for the rest of his life. Considering the man had, more than likely, never done an honest day's work in the past, it was inconceivable. For now, he refused to dwell on anything so negative. He needed to concentrate on the scheduled meeting with the three youngsters.

~ * ~

People from all over the complex milled around the dining area. It always amazed Peter to see how many people from all walks of life lived and worked there. It was easy to tell the aliens from the earthlings even though they comingled with great ease.

After deciding on what they wanted to eat, Peter and Radon made their way to one of the large tables at the back of the room. Brad, Dan and Norman were already there, feasting on cheeseburgers and fries, while their mentors were eating much healthier foods.

As soon as Peter and Radon approached the table, the mentors were on their feet, acknowledging the newcomers. It seemed as though the three men considered Radon to be their superior. Just by looking at them, Peter knew they were much younger than Radon, perhaps because they were mentoring younger children.

"Have you had a chance to tell the boys about the plans that are being made for their futures?" Radon asked.

"We were just discussing it," Siner, Brad's mentor, replied.

"I don't understand," Brad complained. "Why can't we stay here?"

Peter could see a difference in Brad as well as hear it in his voice. He was no longer the belligerent youngster he'd met the day before. This morning, he was a child, frightened of what the future could hold.

"Staying here," Peter began, "would be acceptable, but there is a woman at the Denver complex who is working on a counseling program for kids who have been abused. You all have to admit, we were abused by the Hendersons. Some of us more than others."

He looked directly at Brad, knowing he often took punishments meant for the other children his age. Understanding this, he realized the move was more important for Brad than for the other boys. It was true they would all benefit from the counseling Hodia would be able to provide for them.

"What about you, Dan, and Norman? Are the two of you willing to be relocated to Denver?"

"If Brad is going, I'm in," Norman said.

"What about going back to the ranch?" Dan asked. "Will I still be able to learn how to cook?"

Peter watched the expression on Brad's face. Yesterday he'd been skeptical about Dan's desire to learn how to cook. Today he didn't see the same thoughts hidden behind the boy's hazel eyes.

"Whatever any of you want to study or to become will be made available to you at the ranch. We have to get things up and running before we can get the educational programs started."

It surprised Peter how Radon was able to put voice to the answer to Dan's questions. The more he was around his mentor the more he appreciated the alien who had saved his life and given him the correct advice at the appropriate times.

It came as a surprise when it was Norman, who seemed to have replaced Brad as the leader of the group, spoke. "I trust all of our mentors and they have promised they will be coming to Denver with us. My mentor, Draven, told me there are mountains there and we can go hiking in them. He helped me look it up on my communicator. I would like to see those mountains."

Dan agreed, but Brad remained silent. The move was more for his benefit than for theirs. Peter hoped the enthusiasm of both Norman and

Dan would eventually rub off on Brad.

~ * ~

By late afternoon, all of the arrangements had been made for the three boys, their mentors, Peter and Radon to relocate to Denver. They would be taking two large hovercrafts to accommodate all eight of them.

At Peter's request, Brad and his mentor Siner were assigned to his craft. Siner was indeed much younger than Radon and seemed to need Radon's advice.

Throughout the trip, the two aliens were in constant communication with each other. Even though there were no spoken words, Peter knew they were communicating telepathically.

"Are you excited about the relocation?" Peter asked, breaking the silence between himself and Brad.

"I guess so. Norman says we can go hiking in the mountains. I like that a lot better than working in the classroom."

"You do understand why you have to do your schoolwork, don't you?"

Brad nodded. "I do, but it's so hard."

"I can understand what you're saying, but from what I've heard, Hodia has an excellent group of counselors who will help you become more comfortable in the classroom. With any luck, they will be able to come to Resurrection Ranch with us. You aren't the only ones who need their help. Any of us who lived through those horrors need it too. I know I do and so do Clint, Parker and Roger. I worked with them on the ranch in Mexico and we all have emotional scars we need to deal with. With any luck, Ken, Dennis and Jerry will be found and they will benefit from the counseling as well."

"You need counseling? Why?"

"Because I didn't have a normal childhood, and when I went to work on the ranch in Mexico, things were just as bad, if not worse. I'm older and I can understand the need for it. With the proper help, we can all grow from the help these people can give us."

Brad sat quietly for a few moments. "If you think this is best, I will too."

Peter smiled at Brad's confession. There was hope for this young man. He prayed the last three would be as receptive to the idea of what Resurrection Ranch would mean in their lives.

~ * ~

The pilot of the hovercraft announced they would be landing at the Denver docking station and Peter readjusted his seat belt. As he did, he could feel a familiar tension begin in him. He realized the last time he had landed in this docking station it had been to testify against his father.

Even though he knew his father had been taken immediately to the penal colony on the dark side of the moon, he was still apprehensive. Returning to Denver meant many things to him. It was true he would be seeing his friends again, but it was also a fact that the memory of the last time he saw his biological father was at this facility.

As soon as they entered the reception area, Peter was relieved to see not only Chris and Mark, but also his mother and Randy. They were the last people he ever expected to have waiting for him.

"I thought you and Randy were heading back to Canada today," he greeted his mother.

"We were, but when we found out you were transferring here, we decided to stay a few more days to get to see you for a while."

Before he could embrace his mother, he felt a presence close to him. Looking back, he saw Brad inching closer to his side. Instinctively, he knelt down to be on the same level as the boy. "Are you afraid?"

As though he'd gone suddenly mute, Brad nodded.

"This is my mother and my new father. They stayed here to see me before they return to Canada to prepare for their move to Nevada."

"What's it like to have a mother?" Brad said, his voice hardly louder than a whisper.

"I'm the wrong person to ask. I only just found them. I was taken away from my mother when I was very young. I remember how much she loved me and when I found her the love was still there."

Turning toward his parents, he made the necessary introductions.

"Brad is one of the boys whose parents weren't found."

"I'm so sorry," Rita said, also getting down to Brad's level. "I've met the people who will be working with you on Resurrection Ranch, and they are looking forward to meeting you. I think you will be very happy here."

At first Brad seemed to shrink away from Rita's touch. When she withdrew her hand, he actually reached out. It was evident he needed the warmth of a woman's touch. Knowing how the complexes were run, Peter knew Brad's contact had been with men rather than women.

Watching Brad's reaction made Peter wonder if he would see the same behavior from Dan and Norman when they arrived. For some reason he doubted it. Without knowing what punishment Brad had endured at the hand of the Hendersons, he was in the dark as to what was behind his apprehension when he was confronted with a woman for perhaps the first time. Hopefully, meeting with Hodia and her team would bring him out of his shell and help with his rehabilitation.

Within fifteen minutes of their landing, the shuttle carrying Dan and Norman as well as their mentors also landed. Peter watched them closely as they entered the reception area, with the purpose of seeing how they would respond when he introduced them to his parents. Surprisingly, he didn't see the same hesitation he'd seen with Brad only minutes earlier.

He decided something had happened to Brad while he was at the ranch. It was possible whatever it was came at the hands of Mrs. Henderson. He knew she could be cruel, but what had she done to this boy that made him shy away from women, when it was evident he craved their love.

While his parents became acquainted with the new arrivals, Peter made his way to where Chris and Mark waited for him.

"I take it the boy who was with you was Brad," Chris observed. "I saw the way he reacted to your mother. What are you thinking might have prompted his response?"

Before Peter could answer, Mark spoke up. "I think I have an idea. Until I saw Brad's response to Peter's' mom, I'd forgotten some of the things that were done to me while I was at the ranch. One time when I was being punished, it wasn't Mr. Henderson who did the punishing but

Mrs. Henderson. While Mr. Henderson was downright mean, she was sexually abusive. I was relieved never to have to suffer at her hands ever again. Do you think it's possible that's what happened to Brad, not once, but over and over again?"

Peter took a moment to allow what Mark said to sink in. "I don't ever remember anything like that happening to me, but it's possible. We should talk to Hodia and her team about this. Perhaps they could get to the bottom of Brad's behavior and learning disabilities."

Although he wanted to be with Brad, he knew there would be time for that later. For now, he wanted to be with his family. They would be leaving for Canada in the next couple of days and he was certain he wouldn't see them again until everyone was either settled on or around Resurrection Ranch.

"Don't worry about Brad," Chris said, as though he'd read Peter's mind. "Mark and I will introduce him to Hodia and her team. You go and be with your family. We both know and understand the importance of family, especially after everything we've endured. Once you're free, Hodia has some news about Ken, Dennis and Jerry. She's almost certain she has located them, although they're no longer all in the same group. As soon as there is more information, she plans to arrange a meeting between you and them."

Peter was relieved to know Brad would be well cared for while he spent time with his family.

Chapter Seventeen

All too soon, it was time for Peter's family to return to Canada. He'd spent good quality time with them and especially enjoyed the time with his sisters.

To his amazement, both girls were anxious to meet the three boys who came from the Nevada Complex to Denver. It was good to see the boys interacting with children their own age. The girls taught them some games they'd never been able to play while being at Henderson Ranch, such as tag and hide and go seek.

For Peter, these games brought back long hidden memories from when he would go to the daycare center while his mother worked to support them. As much as he missed his mother during the early days at Henderson Ranch, he found he also missed the childhood games he'd once played. He vowed if any other children were brought to the ranch, they would not be deprived of these pleasures.

He stood in the reception area until his family had long since departed. Even knowing they would be reunited within the next few weeks, he knew he would miss them terribly now that they'd departed for Canada.

At last, he made his way to the classroom where he'd been told Hodia and her team were working with Brad and the others. For a moment, he stood outside the room and watched their interaction with the instructors through the one-way glass. He knew from inside the room, it would appear as a mirror.

When they'd first started the classes, Radon told him about the mirror and how people could watch what was going on without being intrusive upon those who were being studied. He wondered if people watched him when he was studying in Mexico City.

He was surprised at how comfortable Brad appeared to be in Hodia's presence. He wondered if there had been a breakthrough during the two days he had spent with his family. The boys all seemed to be comfortable with Peggy and Jenny, but they were also children. They certainly weren't the adults who seemed to frighten Brad the most.

Hodia stood up, indicating the lesson had come to an end. It gave Peter an excuse to enter the room and make his presence known.

"How are your classes going?" he asked.

"Great," Dan and Norman said in unison.

"How about you, Brad? Are things getting better for you?"

"A little, I guess. Miss Hodia has been working with me and making things easier. She's not like Mrs. Henderson. She's also nothing like the teachers at the last place. I can't stay and talk to you now, though. I have to meet with Miss Jerilyn."

"Who's she?" Peter asked, not familiar with the name.

"She's Brad's counselor," Hodia said, joining the conversation. "Once we were made aware of the abuse Brad endured at Henderson Ranch, I knew she was the one counselor to help him the most. She was rescued from an abusive situation about ten years ago and has not only flourished but has also given us great insight into abused children."

"Is she one of your people?"

"If you mean an Alien, no, she isn't. We were told of the abuse by someone who knew of her situation and wanted to help. She was living in an isolated cabin in the mountains with her stepfather. Things went well until her mother passed away and her stepfather treated her more like a wife than a child. She was degraded and made to cook and clean, without being given the opportunity to go to school. Thank goodness we rescued her before the abuse went from bad to worse."

"How old is she?"

"She's a little younger than you. Had she been left in his care much longer, who knows what would have happened. Thankfully, she was allowed to mature under our care. Once she finished her initial education, she decided she wanted to become a counselor. I have to admit, she's been invaluable to us, especially now that the three children you bought to us have arrived."

"Where are they having these sessions? Is it possible for me to monitor their interaction, like I could when I watched the children having their lessons with you?"

"Unfortunately, no one is able to monitor their sessions. What is said between Jerilyn and the children she is counseling is privileged information. I can make the arrangements for you to meet with her after their session is ended. At that time, anything she tells you will be in the strictest confidence."

Peter nodded. He understood completely. There were things he told Radon about the abuse he endured at both Henderson Ranch and the slave ranch in Mexico that he wouldn't want anyone else knowing, especially his friends or his family. It was enough that people who knew him were aware of the brand on his upper arm saying he was the property of Señor Alfanso. Anything else that happened to him was the subject of his worst nightmares.

~ * ~

Peter was sitting in the dining area when a lovely young woman approached his table. It was obvious she wasn't one of the aliens. Her hair hung loosely around her shoulders and was a rich chestnut in color. As she got closer to his table, he could tell her eyes were brown with gold flecks, rather than the distinctive violet of the aliens.

"Are you Peter?" she asked.

He got to his feet and held out his hand to her. "Guilty as charged. You must be Jerilyn."

"I am. Hodia said you wanted to talk to me about Brad. I'm afraid there's not much I can tell you, though. I'm certain Hodia told you about the need for our sessions to remain private."

"She did. I wanted to meet you because of the change I saw in Brad this afternoon when I monitored his classroom. I also wanted to know if you would be interested in counseling older survivors of Henderson Ranch."

"If you're talking about Chris and Mark, I've met with them both and they are surprisingly well adjusted considering the childhood they survived."

Peter held out a chair for Jerilyn and waited until she seated herself before pushing up his sleeve so she could see the brand that mirrored the ones burned into the rumps of the cattle on the Alfanso Ranch.

"I'm thinking more of myself. I'm certain there are things I've endured that have scarred me, like this has."

She gasped when she looked at the brand that would always be a reminder of his days as a slave working for Señor Alfanso.

"Is that what I think it is?" she asked, reaching out to touch the ugly scar that would always be with him.

"Yes, it is. This is the brand for all of the stock owned by Señor Alfanso. Be they cattle, horses, or human slaves, everyone carried the same brand, saying they were bought and paid for by the master of the ranch. There will be four of us at Resurrection Ranch with the same brand."

"That's absolutely inhumane. I thought my childhood was horrible, but at least my stepfather never branded me. Does anyone else know about this?"

"Everyone who knows me, but this was the least of the atrocities that I lived through from the time my father kidnapped me until I was rescued by my mentor, Radon, and his people. Even at my father's trial, I didn't tell people what I'd lived through. It was far too hurtful, not only to me but also to my mother and my new family. I wouldn't want them to ever know what my life was like."

"Does your family know about the brand?"

"Of course, they do. It's not something I can hide from them. It was best I told them how I came by being branded by my owner. It's some of the other things I need to work through."

"I think we could find some time to meet, but you seem quite well adjusted to me."

"What you see is on the outside. I continue to have nightmares and wake up wondering if I'm still stuck in that situation."

"We could start by sharing the evening meal tonight. I could see the chefs were getting ready to start serving and I'm certain we could find a secluded table where we could talk in private. Of course, if you were to be more comfortable in my office, we could go there after we finish eating."

Peter smiled. Jerilyn suggesting they share a meal was more than he could have hoped for. From the first minute he'd seen her, he knew he wanted to get to know her better and not just as a counselor. He definitely wanted her to become important in his life, but he had no idea how to proceed. Perhaps as his counselor, something more could come of it.

~ * ~

Jerilyn had been hearing about Peter ever since he first arrived at the Denver complex for the trial of his father. She admitted, if to no one but herself, he intrigued her. When Hodia told her, he'd asked to meet with her privately, she'd been thrilled, excited and at the same time a bit frightened about having a face to face with him.

Her background, with the abuse of her stepfather, made her wonder if she was fit company for any man. Since being rescued, she knew her calling was to be a counselor to other abused children. She'd never had any feelings for the young men who came to the complex before, but Peter fascinated her.

When she suggested she wanted to share the evening meal with him and accept him for counseling, she knew she needed more. He wasn't one of the abused children she was used to counseling. He was a man in every sense of the word.

The brand he carried on his upper arm attested to the horrors he'd endured during his life. She prayed she would be able to guide him through the process of accepting what he could never change and look forward to the future.

Her assumption of the evening meal being ready to be served was correct. After choosing their food, Peter led them to a secluded table for two in the far corner of the dining area. Rather than delve deeply into their past lives, they talked about the plans that were in the works for Resurrection Ranch.

"Hodia told me you're planning to be the foreman of the new

ranch. Is that all you want out of life?"

Peter raised an eyebrow at her question. "For now, it is. I've been talking to several of the young men and boys we've found with nowhere else to go. I met with Clint, Parker and Roger when we were at the complex near Mexico City together. We were all sold to Señor Alfanso and worked on his ranch until we were rescued. They were receptive to the idea, at least until they can finish their educations and decide what it is they want to do with their lives. After I returned from Canada and my father's trial, I went first to Mexico City and then to the Nevada complex and met with the three kids you've been counseling these past few days. We have three more men we have to contact. I'm told they're in this area. As soon as Hodia and Chris make the arrangements, I plan to meet with Ken, Dennis and Jerry. From what I know, as well as what I've seen, every one of us will need counseling at one point or another. Do you think this is something you'd like to tackle?"

Although she expected the question, it still caught her off guard. "I've been considering it. I know that the children will still need me once they transfer to the ranch, but I hadn't considered taking on so many adults."

From the look on his face, she could tell he was disappointed. Somehow, she would have to show both Peter, and herself, that she was up to the challenge.

"Do you want to go back to my office?" she asked.

A mischievous smile crossed Peter's lips. "I don't think talking in your office would be nearly as much fun as doing the same thing while walking in the gardens. I'm told they're beautiful, especially at night."

"I think that sounds like an excellent idea."

After they took their dinner trays to the kitchen for the dishes to be run through the dish sterilizer, she allowed him to take her hand and lead the way out to the gardens. Within the dome of the complex, beautiful flowers grew and scented the air with a pleasing aroma. Solar lights lined the paths through the rows and rows of delightful blooms.

Without hesitation, Peter started talking about many of his experiences. She was thankful the semi-darkness of the evening hid her expression of shock when he talked about how the private areas of his body had been examined, not only by Señor Alfanso but also by Mrs. Henderson, during his formative years. It was no wonder he told her he had demons he needed to rid himself of. The physical and sexual abuse had been accompanied with verbal abuse, where he'd been told over and over again that his mother, like all other women, was a dirty whore.

Listening to him talk about the things he'd endured brought to mind the years of abuse she lived through with her stepfather. She was now certain her mother's death had been because of the man she now despised more than anyone else on earth.

"You must be a witch," Peter said, breaking into her innermost thoughts. "I've told you things that no other person has ever heard. When Mark first talked about the sexual abuse he suffered at the hands of Mrs. Henderson, I said I didn't remember any such abuse. It wasn't until the memories resurfaced in my dreams that I recalled what she'd done to me."

"As far as I know, I'm not, nor have I ever been a witch. I think it's these gardens. The scent of these flowers is very heady. Perhaps they are the reason you have felt comfortable confiding in me. You must know whatever you tell me is in the strictest of confidence. It is the same as what I have learned from the three children you brought here several days ago. To be truthful, listening to you tell of what you endured has brought back some of my unresolved memories. Would you be surprised to know that I think my stepfather had something to do with the death of my mother?"

Peter stopped and turned to face her. "After everything I learned about my father, nothing surprises me. Is there any way you can find out what actually happened to your mother?"

Tears she hadn't shed in years rolled down her cheeks. "I was very young when my father was killed in a hunting accident. My stepfather was his best friend and within a year he married my mother. They were married for about three years when she got sick and died. I was six or seven at the time. It was so sudden, and I was so young, I never questioned what happened. At that time, he started treating me like his wife. I learned to cook and clean and to pleasure him sexually, by giving him oral sex. Thank goodness I was rescued before I matured enough for him to want me sexually. I guess that's why I am able to understand what you and the others who were brought up to sacrifice my virginity to him."

Peter nodded his head sagely. "As a child, you wouldn't make the connection, but doesn't it seem strange that after your father's 'accidental' death, his best friend married his widow? Add to that the fact she died so suddenly, and it makes you, as an adult, question these circumstances. I think you should talk to Cassion and Hodia about this. Like the crimes committed by my father, it's possible he's more than likely going to kill again. He should be imprisoned for what he did to me, but before he could be taken into custody, he disappeared. No one has heard from him since."

She hadn't thought of it that way before, but it made complete sense. What if her stepfather had killed both of her parents in order to corrupt their child, and make her his lover when she was old enough to be forced to become his sexual partner for the rest of her life?

Before she could respond, Chris joined them.

"I've been looking for the two of you all evening."

The look on Peter's face was one of annoyance at being interrupted, but when he turned to face his friend, it became unreadable almost immediately.

"Has something happened?" Peter inquired. "Is one of the boys sick?"

"Nothing like that," Chris replied. "Hodia contacted me to say the last three of the men we were looking for have been contacted and will be at the complex tomorrow morning. She wants to meet with the three of us to talk about how we are going to approach them. They've been with one of the white supremacist groups and she's not certain how receptive they will be to coming with us to the ranch."

"You were with one of those groups, Chris. What prompted you to leave?" Jerilyn asked.

"Learning the history behind groups like that and realizing what my Native American blood meant to people like them."

"In that case, we will have to enlighten them and see where they stand with their group," Peter added.

Together, the three of them went back inside to meet with Hodia. For Jerilyn, it was bittersweet. She had been certain Peter was going to take her in his arms and kiss her. Having been interrupted, she wondered if they would ever have such a chance again in the future and if they did, would she be as receptive as she was tonight?

Instead of thinking about what might have been, she concentrated on what Peter had said concerning her stepfather. As a child she'd accepted what happened to her natural parents. As an adult, she questioned her stepfather's actions. Tomorrow she would voice her suspicions to Hodia and Cassion.

~ * ~

After their meeting with Hodia, they all returned to their accommodations within the complex. Once alone, Peter relived the evening he spent with Jerilyn in the garden. Earlier he'd called her a witch. Now he wondered how close he'd come to the truth. Never before had he considered having feelings, of this kind, like the ones he harbored for Jerilyn. Had Chris not interrupted them, he would have kissed her. How could that be when he'd been taught all his life that women were whores?

Rather than dwell on Jerilyn or the feelings that were so new to his mind and body, he turned his thoughts to the men he would soon be meeting.

To him, theirs were familiar names, but nothing more. While they were at the Henderson Ranch, he knew them as the older boys. As they all progressed in age, their duties changed. They were always a step ahead of himself and his friends. It was almost as if each age group was segregated, kept away from those who were both older and younger than themselves.

In his mind, he couldn't picture the faces of Ken, Dennis and Jerry. They had already moved on to tasks with more responsibility and were not involved in teaching Peter, Chris and Mark the tasks they would be taking on. That was left to the age group just above theirs, not those who were two years older.

Finally, he decided to put all his apprehension for the future behind him and go to bed for the night. Whatever transpired over the next few days would be tightly monitored by the mentors who had been assigned to each of them.

Chapter Eighteen

It came as no surprise when Peter and Radon found Chris and Mark, along with Cassion and Hodia, waiting for them at a table for six in the dining area.

"Have you eaten yet?" Radon asked.

"No, we were waiting for you," Chris replied. "We have a feeling today is going to be a trying one with the new arrivals. We're not certain what to expect from them and thought you and Peter could use some backup."

Peter breathed a sigh of relief. He'd worried about talking to the men who they would be meeting later in the morning. When he approached Clint, Parker and Richard, he knew they were on equal footing. He knew what they'd endured while working on the slave ranch in Mexico. These men were coming from a different dynamic entirely. He had no idea what their living conditions had been over the past few years. How their minds had been altered. He also didn't know if they had been tortured as he had, or if the torture they encountered was mental rather than physical.

They all went through the buffet line before their conversation continued.

"Do you remember any of these guys?" Mark asked, as he pushed pictures of the three men across the table for Peter to scrutinize.

He looked at the photographs, trying to remember them with younger features. Although they all looked vaguely familiar, he couldn't say for certain that he remembered them. Rather than a verbal answer, Peter shook his head.

"I didn't think so," Chris said. "Being with those hate groups tends to harden you. I should know. I was with them for a couple of years, and it wasn't easy. At the time I thought it was freedom, but I didn't know true freedom until I came here. I was an angry young man when I first met Cassion, Hodia and Caroline. They helped me to find out who I was and where I belonged in this world. We have to do the same thing for these men."

Peter looked more closely at the pictures. Staring at them, he tried to look past the shaved head of one of the group members, as well as the tattoos. The other two men had full heads of hair. It was evident they were no longer considered skinheads.

"What have these guys been through?" he asked, hardly aware he'd voiced his innermost thoughts.

"We're about to find out," Radon said. "I just had a communication that these men are waiting for us in the conference room. Did you say Jerilyn would be joining us this morning, Peter?"

For a moment, Peter had forgotten he'd asked Jerilyn to be with them when they interviewed the newcomers. "Yes, I did. I should let her know where to meet us."

"Did I hear my name mentioned?"

Peter turned to see Jerilyn standing behind him. "I guess you did. The last three men from the ranch that had no one to claim them have been found. We are getting ready to go to the conference room to meet them."

"I know. I was finishing my breakfast when I had a message from Hodia about them. When I saw you over here, I decided to come over and tag along with you."

Peter didn't have to turn back to his friends to know they too could feel the electricity between himself and Jerilyn. "It would be my pleasure to escort you to the conference room, lovely lady."

Behind him, he could hear his friends' snickers, but he didn't care. Jerilyn had some kind of power over him that he didn't understand. He'd only known her for a matter of hours and yet he didn't want to be parted from her for any reason whatsoever.

~ * ~

The conference room was more like the sitting room in a family home. Couches and overstuffed chairs were arranged in a comfortable setting rather than a long meeting table with chairs around it. The mentors, including Hodia, who Peter soon learned was Jerilyn's mentor, stayed to the back of the room, leaving the younger members of the group to get better acquainted.

"I'm Ken Raspier," one of the former skinheads said, extending his hand. "I've been hearing about the raids on Henderson Ranch and wondered if you would come looking for us. Dennis and I left the skinheads several months ago and just persuaded Jerry to join us. Miss Hodia told us about what you're doing and asked if we wanted to join you."

"That about sums it up," Peter replied. "Mark and I were both sold to slave ranches in Mexico and Chris ended up with a group such as the one you were in. After being rescued, Chris and Mark associated themselves with Resurrection Ranch. It's the old Henderson place, but it's going to be run differently. There, we will be running cattle and horses, but we will also all be getting the education we were denied as children."

"Will the aliens be running the show?" Jerry Salinger, the last of the group to leave the skinheads asked, as he nodded toward the mentors who were seated at the back of the room.

It was Chris who answered the question. "I've been training to oversee the educational program while finishing my own education. Mark and Peter will also be continuing their educations while Mark manages the operation, with Peter working as the foreman for the ranch. As for our mentors, they will be there as advisors as well as teachers. We've all found family who want to be involved as well. It's turning into quite an operation."

Dennis Wallace was the next to speak up. "How did you find your families? I didn't think any of us had people who cared for us."

"With each of us it was different," Mark said. "Hodia was the one who found Chris' family. We were at the trial for the Hendersons when the cop who found me after my mom was killed was able to reunite me with my birth family. I took the good with the bad when I realized it was my grandfather who killed my mother. Not only did I meet him and my father, but I found a loving grandmother, a stepmother and a half brother and sister. They are all going to be involved in the project in one way or another. With Peter, it was due to Hodia's research that he found his family."

"Will it be just the six of us?" Ken questioned.

"Altogether there will be twelve," Peter replied. "When I was at the complex in Mexico, I was reunited with Clint Anders, Parker Flint and Roger Blount. They were all sold to the same ranch as me in Mexico. Mark was sold to a different ranch altogether. After I reconnected with my family, I was told there were three kids at the Nevada complex who didn't have family that could be found. I met with them and they are here continuing their education and getting some counseling for the abuse they endured while they were growing up."

It was Jerilyn who spoke up next. "I've also been rescued from an abusive situation by the aliens. It was Hodia who brought me here and is overseeing my education. Through accelerated studies, I have become a licensed counselor. I will be relocating to Resurrection Ranch with everyone else."

Peter stared in amazement at her statement. He'd asked her to come with them to the ranch last night, but she hadn't given him an answer. Was it that she was intrigued by the concept and her ability to be of help, or did she want to be closer to him?

He mentally shook his head, realizing there were more important things for him to consider than his personal life.

"What prompted you to leave the skinheads?" Chris asked, jarring Peter back to the here and now.

"I was the first one to leave," Ken replied. "I wasn't content with the situation. I finally woke up one morning and realized the hate these people were spewing reminded me of the life we lived on Henderson Ranch. I was different, not exactly what Mr. and Mrs. Henderson wanted me to be and not what these people wanted me to be either. I didn't like carrying a gun and hating someone whose skin wasn't the same color as mine. I also realized I wasn't like the others. I fantasized about being with other men and I knew they hated people like me. I finally broke ties with them, with nowhere to go. I hired out on one of the ranches in the area. That was when I started trying to persuade Dennis and Jerry to join me. I might not have book smarts, but I did know how to work a ranch, even though it wasn't exactly what I wanted to do with my life."

"It was pretty much the same with me," Dennis continued. "Ken and I were close friends and kept in contact. We would meet secretively, and I saw how much happier he was. I left a couple of weeks later and got hired on at another ranch close by. That's when we started meeting with Jerry. We finally talked him into leaving as well. Of course, we know we're all on a hit list from the group. They never found out about Ken's sexual persuasion and if they did, they would think Jerry and I were like that too."

Peter was surprised to hear about Ken's homosexuality and how openly he discussed it. He looked to Jerry to continue the story. It was evident he was the youngest of the group.

"I guess it's my turn. After Ken left, there were a lot of threats being made and they got worse when Dennis left. I was at the point that I feared for my life and took off in the middle of the night about a week and a half ago. Ken was there to help me. He said he was going to find me a job like the ones he and Dennis had, but the people from this complex found us first. I was more than happy to come with them. When I got here, I was examined, and I found out I had Asian genes. Had the people in the group ever found that out, I would have been dead years ago."

"So how do you feel about joining our project?" Mark asked.

"I think I can speak for all of us," Dennis began. "We all know ranching. We're also all different. Ken prefers guys and that's okay with me. Jerry has an Asian American background and I'm nothing more than a mutt. With an education, who knows what we will want in the future. What if we don't always want to be ranchers?"

"I understand what you are saying," Peter said. "We want to run the ranch and give everyone the opportunity to become who they are meant to be. With the help of Hodia and the others, you might find family like Chris, Mark and I did. I've been talking to some of the younger kids and one of then already knows he wants to become a chef. Once we get things going, he'll be able to pursue his passion. It will be the same for anyone who wants to go in a different direction."

They talked for over an hour, answering the questions the newcomers posed and putting their minds at ease. It was evident their biggest fears were being found by the group they'd left and eliminated, not only for leaving but for who and what they were.

Finally, it was Cassion who stood to address the group. "We are interested in this project and in giving everyone involved the best protection available. If that means changing your identities, so be it. We have no fears for Chris, Mark, and Peter, as well as the three young men coming from Mexico and the children we brought here from Nevada. They have no enemies since the people responsible for their situations have been tried and convicted. With the three of you, things are different. If you are willing to join us, you will each be given a mentor who will be responsible for not only your education but also your safety. As we speak, Hodia is looking to find if you have any families. She's very good at what she does along those lines and is also one of the best teachers we have."

"What if I'm good at ranching, but I would like to study art?" Ken asked.

"I think I can answer that question," Hodia said, getting to her feet. "I'll be working with Chris to make our educational program one of the best in the country. If you want to study art, we will do our best to find the best instructors available. No one wants to force you into ranching if that's not what you decide to do with your life. We want to have a safe place for any of the former residents who want to come for instruction and counseling. Where your life takes you after that is up to you."

Peter wondered what thoughts were swirling through the minds of the three newcomers. When each of them agreed to come to Resurrection Ranch, he felt a weight lift from his shoulders. With thoughts of what would happen when they contacted the former skinheads taken from his mind, he could concentrate on his life and the woman who had dominated his thoughts for the past day. To hear her say she would be willing to relocate to Resurrection Ranch, he knew his decision to become the foreman while continuing the education he'd been denied, was the right one.

~ * ~

With the meeting completed, everyone went their separate ways. For the newcomers, they were taken to apartments where they would be able to relax and contemplate everything they'd learned during the meeting.

Chris and Melian, as well as Mark and Kara, went out for a walk in the gardens, leaving Peter and Jerilyn to get better acquainted.

"I was surprised when you said you would be joining us at Resurrection Ranch," Peter said, once they were alone. "I only mentioned it to you last night and…"

"Slow down, cowboy, you might have mentioned it last night, but that doesn't mean I didn't know about it before then. I've had some long conversations with Hodia about it. She is my mentor. She suggested I accompany her to the ranch. My mind has been made up for over a week."

"You deceived me," he teased.

"Not really. I just didn't tell you everything I knew. I wanted to sort out my feelings first. I've been obsessed with you ever since I heard you were coming for your father's trial. I wanted to see how I reacted to you in person before I let you in on my plans. I was comfortable with you the moment I saw you, but I wanted to see how you felt first."

Peter laughed at her confession. "I've spent the night with dreams of you. It's amazing because I was always told all women were dirty whores. If I hadn't met my mother and sisters, I don't know how I would have reacted to you. A lot has changed in the last few months. It's hard to take everything in."

"Let me help you," she said, squeezing his hand. "I've been trained as a counselor and I know I can help you. Of course, I don't just want to be your counselor, I want to be so much more."

Before Peter could answer, sirens went off and a voice came over the intercom system. "Warning, this facility is on lockdown. Everyone should return to the facility and do not leave until we can alleviate the threat."

"What do you think is going on?" Peter asked.

As soon as Peter posed the question, Chris and Mark were at his side.

"I'm afraid the skinhead group that our new friends once belonged to have found out they're here," Chris said. "If what they told us is true, their former group members have been searching for them since they left. I went through this when I first came here. The difference is I was on the outside rather than the inside. I was one of them rather than what I am today."

"Are we in danger?" Peter's voice sounded with fear.

"We would be if it weren't for the protective shield. It would have been put in place before the warning came over the intercom system. They're undoubtedly heavily armed. I know when the group I was with came here, we all carried assault rifles and we knew how to use them. We soon learned they were ineffective against the shield. What we need to do is shelter in place and allow the security forces to handle things from here on."

They turned to head back to their apartments, when they were met by Ken, Dennis and Jerry.

"Maybe this wasn't such a good idea. It's us they want," Dennis said.

"It's more like it's you they want," Ken said. "Once they find out I'm gay and Jerry has Asian ancestry they would rather have us dead than with them."

Jerilyn clung to Peter's arm. "I was here when the group Chris was with came to attack the complex. That was a frightening time, but as you see, things turned out for the best. The authorities got the militants to stand down and, so far, we haven't heard anything about them since."

"I know how these groups work," Chris interjected. "We need to talk to the leaders. When we do, it's best if the three of you remain hidden. Go back to your apartments and let the security forces handle things. Since I understand these people, I'll go with them."

"Are you certain?" Ken questioned, concern sounding in his voice.

"Positive. I've been through this and although it's hard not to worry, put your mind at ease, this will end on a good note."

Peter could feel the apprehension from everyone in the group. Once the women, as well as the newcomers, went to their apartments, Peter, Chris and Mark prepared themselves for the meeting that would be inevitable.

Chapter Nineteen

It wasn't until late morning of the next day when the plans for the meeting were finalized. For Peter, the wait was almost unbearable. He wondered what could be taking so long. Why would the militants be so hard to convince to come to a meeting within the complex?

"The meeting is all set for nine tomorrow morning," Chris advised Peter when he arrived at his apartment.

"Are you sure this is going to work?"

"Nothing is set in stone, but it's worth a shot. I know when everything was explained to Patrick's group, they dispersed without any further conflict on their part. I have had communication with Patrick since then. He has disbanded the group and they are in the process of getting the proper education that has been financed by the people at this complex."

"That's a relief. Maybe we should let the others know what's going on. Yesterday I could see a lot of fear in their eyes. Especially in Ken and Jerry. They have the most to lose once their sexual persuasion as well as their ethnic background is revealed to the members of that group."

Together they made their way down to the dining area where they met with Ken, Jerry and Dennis.

"The meeting is set for tomorrow morning," Chris said as soon as Mark joined them, and they were seated at one of the large round tables.

"Why such a long wait?" Ken asked.

"From what I was told, they weren't entirely convinced coming inside the complex was in their best interests. Mark's mentor, Cassion, is a respected attorney within this group. He finally made the leaders of the group understand that meeting with us was perfectly safe. He also got them to stand down and put aside their weapons."

"He must be some litigator to convince them to do something like that," Jerry observed.

Mark laughed at the comment. "Once you get to know Cassion, as well as the other advisors, you'll learn they are extremely compassionate and only have the best interests of the people of this planet in their plans. Had it not been for them finding Caroline Phillips with her knowledge of the history of the United States as well as the rest of the world, we would still be in the dark about what happened in the past."

Jerry nodded his head. "I met with her and she told me of how the Japanese-American citizens were treated during the second World War. She also said, she'd been accessing the archives and learned that in 2020/2021 there were atrocities carried out against the elderly of the Asian/American community because of the fear they were behind the spreading of the pandemic that held the world in its grip. Of course, it's all ancient history, but as far as these groups are concerned, we're still considered second-class citizens."

"I've done a lot of studying of history from the papers Caroline has authenticated," Mark said. "It's not just the Asian-Americans, but several other nationalities that are being considered second-class citizens. From what I've learned, in the early twenty-first century, my family would have also been discriminated against because they came from Mexico. No one is exempt when it comes to hate groups. Even Chris would have been considered inferior because of his Native American ancestry."

All three of the fugitives from the hate group stared in disbelief at what Mark was telling them. They listened intently as several more bits of history were revealed. As though time flew, by the time they finished their discussion, the evening meal was being set up on the buffet line.

After they finished eating their evening meal, they retired to their respective apartments in order to rest up for the meeting the following morning.

~ * ~

Peter was surprised to find Jerilyn waiting for him in the hall outside of his apartment. “How long have you been waiting here?” he asked.

“I was in counseling sessions all day. When I came down for the evening meal, I saw you and your friends. Someone told me you’d been having discussions all afternoon, so I figured you would be coming back to your apartment. I definitely wanted to see you and get your take on what you think might happen tomorrow at the meeting. Hodia told me we would both be able to attend as observers.”

Peter touched the pad to give them access to the apartment. After taking two bottles of water from the refrigeration unit, they went into the living room to take advantage of the comfortable seating the room provided.

“I honestly don’t know what to say. I learned a lot about history when I was with Chris and Mark this afternoon. They’ve been rescued for several months longer than I have and have been given more education about the history of our country as well as our world. I was shocked to hear there has been so much hate over the centuries. I thought the Hendersons as well as Señor Alfanso were the ones who invented it.

“As far as tomorrow is concerned, it’s anyone’s guess what will happen. I hope once things are explained to them, they will take the opportunity to learn more of history and stop looking for the newcomers.”

“I agree,” Jerilyn said, as she snuggled closer to him. “I saw what happened when Chris first came here and broke ranks with the group that was intent on storming the complex. I realize at the time President Addison was here to talk to the militants and he helped a lot. Hodia told me he would be present as a hologram to be able to participate in tomorrow’s meeting. I’ve also been told Caroline and her husband, Aaron, will be there. They will be able to authenticate history. Like the group Chris was with, they are not only asking for the return of Ken, Jerry, and Dennis, they are denouncing history. I think it should be an extremely interesting morning.”

They talked for almost an hour, before Jerilyn returned to her apartment, leaving Peter with even more information to digest before the meeting scheduled for the next morning.

~ * ~

After what turned into a night plagued with dreams of the morning to come, Peter was up early and down for the morning meal before any of the others appeared in the dining area. When he chose what he considered to be a healthy breakfast he returned to the table they'd occupied the afternoon before. It didn't take long before the others joined him, their plates piled high with the nutritious food supplied by the complex.

"Did anyone get any sleep last night?" Dennis asked.

Everyone agreed their nerves had kicked in, keeping restful sleep at bay. "I had a lot of dreams about today's meeting," Ken confessed. "I decided I wanted to be there to meet them."

"Do you think that's wise?" Peter questioned.

"I think Ken is right," Chris agreed. "I remember confronting Patrick with my decision. It was the hardest thing I've ever done, but it was a cleansing sensation. I think Dennis and Jerry should be there, too. Like they said last night, they are the ones the militants want. It's best if they have a chance to clear the air between themselves and the leaders."

They were just beginning to eat their morning meal when the mentors who had been assigned to each of them, arrived to accompany them to the meeting. If they were surprised when Dennis, Ken and Jerry announced they wanted to be included, it did not show.

~ * ~

Jerilyn watched as the militant leaders were led into the conference room. She relived the meeting between the authorities and Patrick Ernst's group. Therefore, she wasn't shocked to see their tattooed bodies as well as their shaved heads. It was a relief to see they were unarmed.

Across the room, a large screen projected the picture of President Addison sitting at his desk in the oval office.

"Who the hell is that?" one of the leaders of the group, who identified himself as Maitland, demanded.

"That's the President Addison," Cassion replied.

"Why the hell isn't he here instead of on that damnable screen? Is he afraid of us?"

"On the contrary. He wanted to be here, but your presence demanded we go into complete lockdown and he would have been unable to land. It's best if he joins us through the hologram ability of the teleconference facilities we have at hand."

"He's not 'my' president," Maitland shouted. "I didn't vote for him."

"Who did you vote for, son?" President Addison asked.

"We are a nation unto ourselves. We don't consider anyone to be above us. Our beliefs tell us there is no need for us to vote for anyone other than our own people. Unfortunately, you pigs don't give us a chance to run for any offices. If you did, things would be different."

"I am hardly above you. I am the leader of this country and whether or not you agree with it, you live within the confines of our borders, making you citizens. As such, you are able to run for any public office you want. It is not the authorities who are keeping you from running for office, it is your preconceived ideas that are holding you back."

For a moment there was silence. It was then that Dennis, Ken and Jerry entered the room. Seeing them, Jerilyn held her breath in anticipation of the confrontation that was about to take place.

"These are the ones we came for," Maitland said. "Let us take them back to our compound so they can be dealt with for their desertion in a fitting manner."

"None of us are going back with you," Ken announced, his voice sounding calmer than Jerilyn thought it would.

"You belong to us, bought and paid for," Maitland countered.

"I've learned a lot since I got away from you. What you're referring to is called slavery and that was abolished almost three hundred years ago. I also know going back with you would be like signing my death certificate. I am no longer able to keep the fact that I'm a homosexual a secret and I know what your policy is concerning people like me."

"You're right, fag. You are no longer welcome in our group, but Dennis and Jerry should both be given back to us."

"Hardly," Jerry shouted. "I am also not anyone you want. I have Asian-American ancestry."

The shocked expression on Maitland's face told Jerilyn he had had no idea of the revelations he'd just heard.

"What about you, Dennis?"

Jerilyn watched Dennis closely. He'd been away from the group for several weeks. How would he reply?

"I left the group of my own free will. There is no way I ever want to come back. We've been offered the opportunity of doing something we know, while we get the education we were denied as children. Perhaps you should speak with Mrs. Phillips and find out the truth about the hogwash you're feeding your recruits. Hate is a terrible thing. The way I see things, education is the key to everything. None of us are worth going to war to get us back. It is entirely possible that you paid Mr. Henderson for each of us, but that doesn't mean we're yours for life. According to what you preach, neither Ken nor Jerry would ever be tolerated in your group. In that case, I don't feel as though I would be acceptable to you either because they are my friends."

Hodia and Jerilyn exchanged glances as they waited for Maitland to respond. The anger radiating from his eyes was enough to put fear in both of their minds.

"Friends," Maitland spat. "No one has friends. You must know that at the drop of a hat they could easily turn on you."

"I doubt that."

This time it was Chris who was speaking.

"It wasn't that long ago when I was affiliated with Patrick Ernst's group. We came to this complex to protest the history that was being uncovered. When we finally heard the truth, a lot of things changed within that group. Mrs. Phillips is right—those who don't know the history of the past are doomed to repeat it."

"So where does that leave us?" Maitland asked.

"I have no doubt the members of your group are ignorant," President Addison replied. "That being said, I would like to offer you and your group the opportunity to continue your educations, at the government's expense. This country needs fine young men like yourselves to keep our society moving forward. If you would be accepting of this, I will be glad to send out one of my representatives to get you started on the right path."

The bravado Maitland showed when he first came into the meeting seemed to have drained from his body. Jerilyn could actually see the light of realization come into his eyes. By the end of the meeting, he agreed to the educational opportunity President Addison was offering.

~* ~

With the meeting ended, Peter returned to his apartment. Although he'd had little to no participation during the meeting, he found it had drained him completely. More than anything else, he wanted to sleep and gain the rest he'd been deprived of the night before.

He had just entered his quarters when his communicator indicated an incoming message. It took all his energy not to ignore the message. He knew if it came through his communicator, ignoring it was completely out of the question.

Although he expected to see Radon's face, he was surprised when the faces of Ken, Dennis and Jerry greeted him.

"Can you meet with us later today?" Ken asked.

"Of course, I can," Peter replied, "but what more is there to say than what we said in the meeting?"

"A lot," Jerry said. "We've talked to Chris and Mark and we want to discuss our abilities and how we can help with the ranch."

Peter breathed a sigh of relief. He'd been certain the message would have been that they decided against going to the ranch with the rest of the men and boys who had been rescued over the past few months.

~ * ~

Everyone was waiting for Peter when he arrived at the meeting room. He tried to read the looks on the faces of the newcomers, but they gave no indication as to what they were going to tell them.

"Don't worry, buddy," Chris told him. "We don't know any more than you do. These guys seem to know something we don't, but I'm sure we're going to find out."

It was Ken who stood up as the spokesperson for the group. "I've been out of the group the longest, so I've had time to think about what I want to do with my life. I know I need an education and if that's what you're offering, I'm ready to do whatever is necessary to help Resurrection Ranch not only survive but to thrive. That said, my forte is not in the ranching end of things. When I went to work on the ranch in Colorado, the boss realized where my potential was. His wife ran an interior decorating business and he persuaded her to take me on as an apprentice. With all the new building that's going on, I would be thrilled to go out there and help, not only with the decorating but also with the building of the new structures on the property. I always was better at carpentry than on ranching."

Once Ken took his seat, Dennis got to his feet. "Unlike my friend Ken, I do enjoy the ranching end of things. I have to admit the idea of an education is intriguing, but not as much as doing something I love. Maybe with an education, my life might go in a different direction. Like Ken, I'd like to go out early and work with the cattle. I'm certain whoever is working the ranch could use the help."

Peter was overwhelmed and encouraged at the same time. The only one left to hear from was Jerry. He wondered if the last of their group would be as receptive to the move as his counterparts. He hadn't been out of the skinhead group long enough to have much experience in the outside world.

"Guess that leaves me," Jerry began. "Within the group we were affiliated with, the cook kept a garden. I soon found I enjoyed helping him grow some of the food we were served and to learn about the herbs he liked growing and using. If whoever will be doing the cooking would be willing to have me help out by planting and tending a garden, I think I would have a lot to offer as well as even more to learn. Of course, the formal education is enticing. I would enjoy learning more about garden plants as well as others that are foreign to me."

"That's great news," Mark said, a broad smile gracing his face. "To be truthful I was worried about what you were going to tell us. We are going to be needing all of your skills. I'm certain my father's ex-wife, who is planning to move to the ranch with my siblings to do the cooking until we can employ a chef, will be appreciative of what you're bringing to the table, Jerry. I actually worried about her doing all of the cooking, but she assured me she could handle it. At least until she can be relieved of those duties, so she can begin teaching on the elementary level."

"I agree with Mark," Chris commented. "I know the people from my Cheyenne family's people would like to have any help they can get. That's a big ranch and as I recall they ran several thousand head of cattle to say nothing of the horses they are raising."

Although both of his friends made comment on what the newcomers told them, Peter remained quiet. Although his family wouldn't be physically on the ranch, they would be helping out. He knew all of their help would be appreciated but in reality, they wouldn't be closely associated with any of the young men on the ranch.

"You're quiet, Peter," Mark said. "What do you think about the proposal these guys are making?"

"I'm a bit overwhelmed. All of this is happening so quickly. The skills you are bringing to the table are more than I ever envisioned. I guess I was also thinking about the role my family will be playing in the daily workings of the ranch. Unlike your families, they will be off site but still looking out for our best interests. I don't know what skills Clint, Parker or Roger will have to offer, but I'm certain we will soon find out. Only time will tell as to where their interests will lead them. It's possible one of them might be interested in accounting. As for the little kids, I think Dan would be perfectly paired with Jerry. He wants to learn how to cook, and the way I see it learning about how to grow food at the same time will be a great bonus for both of you."

Peter watched the expression on Jerry's face. He had been the hardest of the group to read. It was evident the thought of having one of the younger boys to teach about gardening while they both learned the art of cooking intrigued him.

"When can I meet Dan?" Jerry asked.

Peter liked the enthusiasm in Jerry's voice. "It can be arranged for tomorrow after he's finished with his classes. I'll talk to his mentor, Felton, and set up the meeting. I remember when I met with Dan, he was skeptical about telling me he wanted to learn to cook. I have a feeling he thought he wouldn't be accepted at the ranch if he had no interest in working with the cattle and horses."

"I know how he feels," Jerry commented. "I worked with the men on the cattle ranch, but I never enjoyed it. Don't get me wrong, I loved riding the horses, but the cattle were another subject. They could turn on you at any minute. I saw one of my friends gored to death by an angry bull. I was probably about twelve years old at the time, and it became the subject of many of my nightmares until I aged out of the program."

Across the table, Chris nodded in agreement. Even though they'd been too young to have seen or even remembered the incident Jerry referred to, they'd heard the stories about it. They knew those stories were told to frighten the boys into being careful around the cattle and to be ever vigilant.

~ * ~

With the meeting ended, Peter sought out Jerilyn. He needed to talk to her and discuss what they'd learned from the newcomers.

He found Jerilyn coming out of her office. From the look on her face, he realized she'd had a trying session with Brad. He was certain the boy could prove to be a handful in the future, unless Jerilyn could make some progress with him.

"How did your meeting go?" she asked when she saw him waiting for him.

"I should be asking you the same question. Is Brad receptive to the counseling you're giving him?"

"You're changing the subject, but yes, I do think he's getting to the point of accepting the fact we'll be with him both here and once we all relocate to the ranch. I also had a chance to talk to Dan today. I won't be meeting with Norman until tomorrow."

"What's your take on Dan?"

"He's a sensitive child. I was surprised when he told me of his desire to learn how to cook."

"I'm glad he told you about that. In meeting with the newcomers, I learned that Jerry is interested in gardening and cooking healthy meals. I'm planning to introduce the two of them tomorrow. I think, even without an education, he has a lot to teach Dan. I hope the two of them will be good for each other."

Jerilyn nodded in agreement. "What about the other two men, Dennis and Ken. I know you told me about Ken being gay. How will he fit in with the rest of them?"

"They all want to leave as soon as possible for the ranch. Ken signed on with one of the ranches in the area close to the militant group. The wife of the owner was an interior decorator and he worked as an apprentice with her company. He wants to help with the decorating of the new facilities that are being built. He's also interested in art. Dennis is actually looking forward to helping with the cattle and horses. Of course, you know about Jerry. They all think they can be of more help there than starting their educations here. They also know they will be expected to continue their education once the classes are set up at the ranch."

"It sounds like everything is coming together. That said, let's see if we can get better acquainted. We'll be working closely once we relocate to the ranch. We know so little about each other, I think some alone time is what we need."

Peter smiled. When it came to relating to Jerilyn, he knew she was far more advanced than he was in education and her experience in counseling put him at a bit of a disadvantage. As much as he wanted her in his life, would her superiority over him work against him? He hoped not.

Chapter Twenty

With Chris and Melian's wedding over, Peter and Jerilyn prepared for their relocation to Resurrection Ranch. Mark and Kara had left several days earlier. Dennis, Ken and Jerry had been at the ranch for several weeks, leaving Jerilyn and Peter to escort the younger boys there.

Peter worried about the responsibility, but Jerilyn promised him everything would go smoothly. She told him even Brad seemed more settled than he had been when he first arrived at the Denver complex.

After packing the last of his belongings, Peter was surprised when his communicator indicated he had a message. Thinking it was Jerilyn reprimanding him for being so slow with his packing, he answered without checking the caller. It came as a surprise when the face of his Canadian lawyer filled the screen.

"Is something wrong?" he asked.

"You might say that. Your father was killed by another inmate at the penal colony. Before he left to go there, he contacted us and said if anything happened to him, all of his assets were to go to you. We've deposited them into your account and are in the process of making investments that will bring you a good return, including one to Resurrection Ranch, through your family. We thought you should be informed."

Peter fought hard to get any words past the lump in his throat. Even though his father had sold him like any other commodity, he was still the man whose seed had taken hold to make him. He didn't have to ask if his mother knew of this new development. If the investment made to Resurrection Ranch went through his new father's firm, she would know what precipitated the donation.

"Thank you," he finally managed to say. "I understand his assets were substantial. Is there enough to compensate the families of his victims? At least the ones we know about."

"There is. We were anticipating this would be something you might want. We have been researching the families and have been able to locate relatives for everyone but Delos Reynolds. From what we've learned, he was an orphan who had no one but your father in his life. Now that we have your decision on this, we will begin to make money available to the families. You are a very generous young man."

The conversation ended with Peter pondering the last words his lawyer said to him. Was he generous, or guilty about the crimes his father perpetuated over the years since taking him away from his mother?

The automated voice announced Jerilyn was wishing entrance into his apartment. Glad to have something to take his mind from his father's death and the people who died at his hands over the years, he let her in.

"Are you ready to leave?" Jerilyn asked as soon as she entered the apartment.

"I just finished packing and was going to come down to meet you, but I had a call from the lawyer in Canada. My father was beaten to death at the penal colony. They wanted me to know about it and to also know that I've inherited his assets, including a sizeable investment into Resurrection Ranch. I've been worried that I don't have enough to bring to the table. I mean, Chris' Cheyenne family purchased the ranch and Mark's family is investing in other ways. I was beginning to feel inadequate."

Jerilyn scowled at his statement. "You are in no way inadequate. Your expertise at ranching, to say nothing of the involvement of your family, is quite an asset, at least from my perspective. Your problem is that you don't give yourself enough credit. I doubt anyone else would have been able to connect with the nine men and boys that were found in the same way you did. Don't ever underestimate your people skills. I've seen them firsthand and even though you are planning to be the foreman, you will play an important part in the prosperity of the ranch."

Jerilyn's confidence in him did much for bolstering his own self-worth. He marveled at how she had entered his life and was now becoming so important to him.

~ * ~

The hovercraft flight from the Denver Complex to Resurrection Ranch was interesting to say the very least. The three boys Peter had first met at the Nevada complex were much further along in the educational process and full of questions.

Dan, who Peter considered to be the most vulnerable, was now the most vocal of the group. He was anxious to reconnect with Jerry. He was excited about being able to begin working not only in the garden, but also in the kitchen with Mark's stepmother.

"When do you think we'll get there?" Dan asked, as he looked out the window of the craft.

"By my calculations, it should be about another forty-five minutes," Peter said.

Of the group, he had the most experience with hovercraft travel. Even with all of her confidence, Jerilyn confided that she'd only flown in a hovercraft once in her life, when she was rescued from her stepfather many years earlier. At least in this one area, he had more expertise than she or the children possessed.

Looking around the group, Peter found Brad to be the most subdued. It came as a surprise, because he remembered the belligerent child that he'd first met weeks earlier.

"Will you be my boss?" Brad finally asked.

"Not until you're old enough to start riding with the men."

"I was riding with the men before they raided the ranch. Why can't I do that now?"

It was Jerilyn who answered his question. "Because, for now, your education is of the foremost importance. When you are in recess from your studies, you will be free to ride the horses or do other things that interest you. As far as working the ranch is concerned, if that is where your interests are, you will be allowed to ride with the men when you're sixteen. You will, at that time, be able to pursue whatever avenue of study you deem important as your life path. Nothing says you have to stay on the ranch or have to leave it. Everything will be up to you."

The expression on Brad's face was one of bewilderment. Peter was certain the boy thought he would have to do the manual labor he'd been forced into for the past several years of his life.

No more had the thought passed through his mind, than the ranch came into view. Peter wasn't certain what he expected to see, but it certainly wasn't the ranch as he remembered it. The old dormitory, as well as many of the outbuildings, had been demolished, leaving sleek new modern ones in their place. The dusty dooryard had been landscaped with colorful rocks and native cactus plants.

As they made their descent, Peter recognized Mark, Ken and Jerry waiting for them to land. It came as no surprise that Dennis wasn't there, as it was early afternoon, and he was certain the hands would be out with the herd.

Thinking about the job he was about to undertake, he was anxious to meet the men from the Cheyenne reservation who had been doing the work for the past several months. Earlier he'd been informed about the arrival of Clint, Parker and Roger. He was certain they were also at work with the other men, since the educational process wouldn't be starting until Chris and Melian returned from Antarctica to begin their administration of the school with Hodia.

As soon as they landed, the boys were ready to leave the craft. It was Jerilyn who persuaded them to wait until she and Mark, as well as Radon, deplaned. Each boy would leave with their mentor. Although she knew they were anxious to explore the ranch where they'd grown up, she decided to make them wait until the adults were reunited with their friends.

"From what I saw from the air, this place looks fantastic already," Peter said when he greeted Mark.

"It's coming along," Mark replied. "I have to say, Ken has been invaluable with the work on the new dormitory and the apartments."

"Did the boys come with you?" Jerry asked.

"They certainly did. Dan is so excited to be able to work with you, at least until the school year starts in earnest. Have you been able to work with Mark's stepmother?"

"I have. Diane is fantastic. Wait until you taste the meals she makes. It's the best food I've ever eaten and I'm learning from her as well. She's really excited to have Dan learning how to cook as well. She says the more hands she has the less work she has to do. I can understand that. She's got a lot of people to feed here. Of course, the new industrial kitchen that was put in is a great help. I guess we have you to thank for that."

"Me?" Peter questioned.

"Your mom said it was their contribution to the ranch. She insisted on having a dining hall with a modern kitchen put in, so Diane had a decent place to work. She said it wasn't right for Diane to be cooking for so many people in the kitchen of her home. Of course, it will be necessary once we get a permanent chef."

Peter was pleased to think his mother had taken such an interest in Resurrection Ranch. What he wondered was where the money came from to finance such a large project. Since he hadn't heard of the death of his father until earlier in the day, he knew the funds hadn't come from that source. He made a mental note to be sure to ask his mother about the generous donation when he saw her.

As the children left the hovercraft with their mentors, it was Dan who broke into a run as soon as he saw Jerry waiting for them.

Peter smiled to see the bond that had started to grow between the two of them at the Denver complex.

"Can we see the garden and the kitchen?" Dan blurted out.

"Soon," Jerry promised. "First we need to get you settled into the dormitory. Your room is on the third floor. I checked it out last night and Dennis did a great job in decorating it. I think you'll like it."

"Will my mentor be there with me?"

"Until you are acclimated to your new lifestyle, he will have a room adjoining yours. After that, he will be able to move into one of the new apartments. A few of them are completed, but there's still a lot of work that has to be done before they're ready for people to move in."

Peter monitored their conversation and realized he had no idea where he would be living. Rather than asking, he took a moment to look around the grounds. Everything was different from the place where he was taken so many years earlier.

Instead of the frightening place he remembered, his surroundings were welcoming. He was anxious to get on the back of a horse and ride out to check on the cowboys who were doing the work he'd done as a child before he aged out of the program.

"Who all is living in the dormitory?" Peter asked.

"On the first floor are you and me," Mark began, "along with Ken, Dennis and Jerry. Of course, as soon as Kara and I get married, we'll be moving into one of the apartments. On the second floor are Clint, Parker and Roger, as well as their mentors."

"Where do the cowboys from the reservation live?"

"They have a bunkhouse in another area of the ranch. Until we get married, Kara and Jerilyn will be sharing an apartment. After the wedding, the apartment will belong to Jerilyn. Not all of the apartments are finished, but there are enough done for Hodia and Cassion, Caroline and Aaron and their son, as well as Chris and Melian. By the time Dr. Gratan and Lego get here next week, their accommodations will be finished as well."

"It sounds like everything is under control. I know your stepmother, as well as your siblings, have arrived. What about your grandmother?"

"She got here last week and is living in the main house with the rest of the family. Once we get everything under control, my uncle, who is a veterinarian, will be arriving to oversee the building of the Vet Clinic as well as the school. I won't be ready to start my studies in that area for at least another two years. That will give us time to find out if any of the others are interested in learning to become vets. In the future, we hope to attract more veterinarian students and turn one, if not two floors of the dormitory into rooms for the post-grad students."

"It sounds like you have everything under control. I'm excited to get started."

"I know how you feel," Mark agreed. "Let me give you the tour while the mentors get the boys settled. We can meet up with them tonight for the evening meal."

Peter smiled to see Dan and his mentor, Felton, following Jerry to the dormitory. Behind them, Norman and Brad, along with their mentors, fell into formation. Although Peter worried about the younger children, he was anxious for the tour Mark promised. He especially wanted to check out the horses and choose one for himself.

Although he'd enjoyed his role in finding and persuading the other nine men and boys to join them, he knew his true love was working with the cowboys as well as the cattle and horses. Even with attending his classes, he was first and foremost the foreman of the operation that would soon prove to be a very profitable endeavor for all of them.

Chapter Twenty-One

Peter marveled at everything that had been accomplished at the ranch before his arrival. He understood he wasn't responsible for anything but the cowboys. That said, he did enjoy the fruits of everyone's labors.

"There's something I wanted to talk to you about," Mark said, as they toured the various buildings.

"Something? That sounds ominous."

"It's not but it is important. I know you told us the man who brought you here was Delos Reynolds, and he was later found murdered. Once we got here, we started looking into the files the Hendersons kept on everyone who came through here as children. One of the first kids to age out of the program was Delos. It seems like he was one of Henderson's pets. When he aged out of the program, he was allowed to go out on his own. That was how he knew to bring you here. The way the records read, things weren't as bad for the first kids who came. It wasn't until the Hendersons realized what a gold mine they had between the free labor from the kids and the money from the state that they figured out they could make even more by selling them to the slave ranches in Mexico, as well as the skinhead groups around the country."

Peter knew his expression had to be one of disbelief. In his wildest imagination he never thought Delos would have been brought up here. Only hours earlier, he'd been told Delos was an orphan. He should have linked that information with the fact the man knew about the ranch when he sold him to the Hendersons.

"From the look on your face, I can tell this information is as overwhelming to you as it was to me."

"It certainly is, but it all makes sense. I often wondered how he knew about this place. Of course, my father was only using him. Once he was no longer of use to him, he turned to murder to shut his friend up. At that point, he was the only one other than my father who knew where I was, and he'd become more of a liability than an asset. It's no wonder that old bastard decided to eliminate him from his life."

"Speaking of your father, have you heard how he's doing at the penal colony?"

"I heard from my Canadian lawyers this morning that he'd been beaten to death by another inmate. Before he left for the dark side of the moon, he had made some arrangements for me to inherit his assets if something should happen to him. I haven't seen any of the numbers, but from what I'm told, my inheritance is substantial. They told me they would make a donation in my name to the ranch, through my parents accounting firm. Before I left the complex in Denver, I asked the lawyers to make some of the money available to the families of his victims. It was then that I learned about Delos being an orphan."

Mark was silent for a moment. It was evident he had no idea of what had been going on in Peter's life.

"I'm sorry to hear that. You've had a lot to digest in a short time. I wondered about the donation from your parents. Since it came in weeks ago, it's definitely not from your inheritance."

"I know they were planning to sell their property in Canada. It's a large estate. It could be they made a good profit from it and used that as the donation to the ranch for the dining hall as well as the kitchen. I'll be anxious to talk to them about it."

Peter could feel hunger beginning to gnaw at his stomach. He'd eaten a good breakfast but a light lunch. By the position of the sun, he realized it was time for them to make their way to the dining hall to enjoy the evening meal.

~ * ~

The dining hall filled quickly with copper-skinned cowboys as well as the former residents who were now getting acquainted with the new look of the ranch.

Peter enjoyed the atmosphere of the room. It reminded him of the dining halls at the alien complexes he'd visited since his rescue. Everything was modern and looked more like an upscale restaurant than a nondescript room. Like the food at the complexes, everything was served buffet style. Tonight, the menu included roast beef with all the trimmings. The mashed potatoes were fluffy and swimming in rich brown gravy. The vegetables were in a butter sauce and the beef was some of the most tender meat he'd ever eaten.

"My compliments to the chef," Peter said when he was introduced to Diane.

"Cooking is much easier in this new kitchen and with all the help I've been getting from Jerry. I also met Dan this afternoon and can hardly wait until I can start training him to help as well. Between all of you boys, you've done a great job putting everything together here. I can see nothing but success in the future. Of course, once we find a chef to take over these duties, I'll be free to work at the school."

Peter beamed at the compliment. He knew it would take a lot of work, but it wouldn't be long before Resurrection Ranch would be a name to be respected throughout the country and perhaps the world.

Coming January 2022
at
Rogue Phoenix Press

Resurrection in a New World
The New World Book Four

Chapter One

Diana Cruz applied her makeup carefully to cover the bruises she'd received days earlier at the hands of her husband, Stephen Cruz.

Thinking back on that night, she remembered putting the finishing touches on the evening meal. Stephen would be home soon and she wanted everything to be perfect. Earlier she'd insisted her teenage children eat an early supper and go to their rooms to do their homework.

Tonight, was special. It was their wedding anniversary. She'd planned the evening down to the last detail. As soon as he walked through the door, she lit the candles she'd placed on the table earlier in the afternoon.

"What the hell is all this shit about?" Stephen raged when he came in the door and saw the candle lit dining room.

"It's our anniversary, I made a special meal for us," she simpered, her words hardly louder than a soft whisper.

"Speak up, bitch."

She pulled herself together. "I said it's our anniversary. I…"

He cut her sentence short with a slap that sent her reeling.

"I don't smell any enchiladas. Are you so stupid that you don't know what day it is? We always have enchiladas on Tuesday. What in the hell were you thinking? You know I don't like all this fancy shit. I also like to see what I'm eating, so put out those stupid candles and turn on some lights so we can eat like civilized people."

Before she could douse the candles and turn on the lights, he attacked her beating her about her face and upper body. With his rage depleted, he helped Diana to her feet.

"I guess I lost my temper. It's too late to make anything else, so we'll eat this slop that you prepared. I'll turn on the lights and blow out the candles while you serve me."

It took all of her energy to walk into the kitchen. As she picked up the silver tray she'd planned to use, she caught a glimpse of herself. Bruises were already forming and blood trickled from her nose. At the sink she washed her face and staunched the flow of blood with cold compresses before she loaded the tray with green salads and assorted bottles of dressing. With the steaks cooking on the indoor grill, she took the salads into the dining room to serve Stephen.

An icy cold settled between them as they ate their salads. The alarm on the grill made her jump up from her chair to get the steaks and baked potatoes to bring to the table. She had no doubt the steaks would be done to a perfect medium rare, as the grill built into the stove always cooked food to perfection.

Once she sat his steak, in front of him, he tentatively cut into it as if expecting it to be either over or under cooked. He examined the piece of meat he'd speared with his fork. Even though she knew there was nothing to be concerned over, she cringed, half expecting to receive yet another beating.

At times like these she wondered why she put up with it, but she knew it was because she loved Stephen with all her heart. He was the father of her children and she had no desire to break up their family.

An alarm on her communicator alerted her to a message that was coming in. As soon as she tapped the screen, her husband's face came into view.

"Call my lawyer," he said without giving her a proper greeting.

"Why?" she questioned.

"The cops just came and arrested me at my office. They gave me some trumped-up charges. Just do as I tell you, bitch." With that he ended the communication.

Panic set in as she frantically looked through Stephen's desk for the number for his lawyer. It took what seemed like hours, rather than the actual minutes it took for her to find the number and make connection with the lawyer.

"Stephen has been arrested," she told the lawyer.

"What are the charges?"

She sat quietly for a moment, as she realized she had no idea what her husband had been charged with. If he told her, she didn't remember.

"I don't know," she finally replied. "He just wanted me to call you. I'm sure you will figure it out once you get down to the station."

For the rest of the day, she worried about what was going on at the police station. The call didn't come through her communicator until just before the kids were due home from school. Even then it didn't come from Stephen but from his lawyer.

"I'm sorry to tell you this, but he's being charged with kidnaping, taking a minor across state lines and abuse. They are recommending he be held without bail until it's time for the trial."

Although Diana put on a brave face while talking to Stephen's lawyer, once he broke the connection, she allowed her tears to flow freely. Somehow, she was going to have to tell her kids what happened today. She knew it would change all of their lives forever.

Also by the Author
at
Rogue Phoenix Press

Awake in a New World
The New World Book One

Caroline Lewis feels life isn't worth living when she loses her husband to Covid-19 while on a business trip to China. In order to avoid the coming pandemic, she opts to have her body frozen to be awakened in 2070. In 2120, archaeologists exploring the ruins of Los Angeles, find Caroline's perfectly preserved body. As she is brought to life, fifty years later than expected, she is forced to learn to live in a world unlike the one she remembers from 2020. Aaron Phillips knows Caroline is special when he hires her as a research volunteer at the library. He hopes she feels the same way about.

Unwanted in a New World
The New World Book Two

Orphaned at birth, Christopher is sent to a ranch for unwanted children. When he ages out, he is embraced by a militant group of skinheads who are unaware of his Native American heritage. A protest at an Alien Complex outside of Denver, opens a new path for his life. While he is receiving his education, his new friends and mentors are working behind the scene to find his birth family.

Melian has come to the complex from the Alien base under the Antarctic ice cap. She takes an immediate interest in Christopher, who now wants to be called Chris, and looks forward to see what their future holds.

Alone in a New World
The New World Book Three

As a child of four, Marco is all alone in the world. With only his mother in his life, her death prompts the authorities to send him to Henderson Ranch for boys. At the age of eighteen, he is sold into slavery to a ranch in Mexico. Two years later, he is recued and reunited with his childhood friend, Christopher. At his friend's insistence he modernizes his name to Mark and embarks on a journey that will bring him full circle back to Henderson Ranch, now called Resurrection Ranch. On his journey, Mark finds previously unknown family and love with one of the alien nurses, Kara, all of whom are willing to journey with him into the future at Resurrection Ranch.

The Return of the Ancients
The Aliens Book One

Nina is devastated when she realizes she must leave Plantas along with the man who is to become her mate, Ragnar, and her best friend, Tarena. When Nina arrives on Earth in Peru at the Nazca plains, she is greeted by a young archaeology student, Rand Jacobson. Even though she is attracted to Rand, she is still grieving the loss of Ragnar.

Ragnar is surprised when, after being greeted as a god on the planet Seros, the military opens fire on his family. After being taken prisoner, he is treated like a lab rat until a scientist, Geni, comes to his rescue. At her estate, he learns the physicians who work with her have saved the lives of his family and friends.

My Uncle the King
The Aliens Book Two

When three contingencies took off from their dying planet, Plantas, only two arrived at their destination unharmed. When the lost contingency is hit with a meteor storm, only one ship survives and makes it to their destination of Nalo. Over the generations, the descendants of the original refugees become the ruling class of their adopted planet. Even the rebel group, the Pure Of Nalo, are unable to unseat the monarchy. When relations with Earth are established, it is Prince Nicos who leaves Nalo to find love on an alien planet and bring back new ideas as well as his Earthly family to save the throne and the people of Nalo.

You Again

While attending college at the University of Wisconsin in the 1960s, Carole Martinson fell in love and eloped with Phillip Vanderlin. When his parents realized she was a farmer's daughter and below them socially, they insisted they divorce.

Fast forward to 2019 and Carole is invited to a wedding cruise financed by her granddaughter's fiancé's grandfather. With no knowledge about the groom's family, Carole flies to Florida for the cruise she and her second husband never got to take. Upon her arrival, she immediately recognizes Phillip.

Phillip never forgot his first love. He is thrilled when he realizes the grandmother is the girl he was forced to leave behind so many years ago.

About the Author

At the age of fifteen, Sherry Derr-Wille walked into her sophomore English class and fell in love with writing. Her teacher, Earl Brockman, “The Duke of Earl,” announced that anyone getting an A on the first test could sit in the back of the room and write for a year. Since no one told her to stop, she continued to write for over forty years before becoming published in 2003.

Married to her high school sweetheart, Bob, for over fifty years, she calls him a saint for putting up with a cray writer. In other words, “you don’t have to be crazy to write a book, but you’re certifiable when you write over eighty of them.” Together they raised three children, have nine grandchildren and six great grandchildren.

Born a country girl, she loves living in a mid-sized city close to the Illinois border with Wisconsin. Being retired gives her time to follow her hear writing, along with editing for several private clients and Rogue Phoenix.

www.ingramcontent.com/pod-product-compliance
Lightning Source LLC
LaVergne TN
LVHW010617100826
845148LV00014B/3013

* 9 7 8 1 6 2 4 2 0 6 4 2 9 *